THE STOWAWAY SOLUTION

GORDON KORMAN TAKES YOU TO THE EDGE OF ADVENTURE

ON THE RUN

BOOK ONE: CHASING THE FALCONERS

BOOK TWO: THE FUGITIVE FACTOR

BOOK THREE: NOW YOU SEE THEM, NOW YOU DON'T

BOOK FOUR: THE STOWAWAY SOLUTION

DIVE

BOOK ONE: THE DISCOVERY

BOOK TWO: THE DEEP

BOOK THREE: THE DANGER

EVEREST

BOOK ONE: THE CONTEST

BOOK TWO: THE CLIMB

BOOK THREE: THE SUMMIT

ISLAND

BOOK ONE: SHIPWRECK

BOOK TWO: SURVIVAL

BOOK THREE: ESCAPE

www.SCHOLASTIC.com

www.GORDONKORMAN.com

GORDON KORMAN

ON THE RUN
CHASE #4

THE STOWAWAY SOLUTION

AN
APPLE
PAPERBACK

SCHOLASTIC INC.
New York   Toronto   London   Auckland   Sydney
Mexico City   New Delhi   Hong Kong   Buenos Aires

No part of this publication may be reproduced, stored in a retrieval system, or transmitted in any form or by any means, electronic, mechanical, photocopying, recording, or otherwise, without written permission of the publisher. For information regarding permission, write to Scholastic Inc., Attention: Permissions Department, 557 Broadway, New York, NY 10012.

ISBN 0-439-65139-5

12 11 10 9 8 7 6 5 4 3 2 1   5 6 7 8 9 10/0

Printed in the U.S.A.   40

First printing, October 2005

For the Lee family,
Alex, Marguerite, and Alexia

"Mr. Bass — your son is on line two."

Mitchell Bass, the well-known Washington attorney, picked up the receiver. "Jonathan — is everything okay?"

"It's not Jonathan," declared a voice that was both shaky and determined. "It's Aiden — Falconer."

Falconer.

It was a name wrenched from the top stories of CNN. Doctors John and Louise Falconer, the husband-and-wife criminologists convicted of treason. The charge: aiding and abetting foreign terrorists.

Mitchell Bass had been their lawyer. He had tried — and failed — to prove that the Falconers had been working for the CIA.

Bass drew in a breath. Fifteen-year-old Aiden Falconer was a fugitive from justice. He and his eleven-year-old sister, Meg, had escaped from a prison farm for young offenders. They had been eluding the juvenile authorities, the FBI, and more than a dozen state and local police departments for more than two weeks.

"Aiden — " he managed. "Where are you? Is Meg with you? The FBI said you were in California — "

The voice on the phone was suddenly sharp, wary. "You talked to the FBI?"

"They called me," Bass explained. "They thought you might try to contact your parents' lawyers. Aiden, listen to me — I talked to your parents, too."

All at once, the teenager's tone softened. "How are they?"

"Worried sick," the lawyer said honestly. "They're more concerned about you two than they are about prison. Both of them begged me to convince you to turn yourselves in."

There was hesitation on the other end of the line. "Turn ourselves in . . ." Aiden mused.

"Give me that phone!" There was a brief struggle, and then an angry voice — a young girl's — declared, "No way, Mr. Bass. If that's what you're thinking, forget it. The next cops we hang around will be the ones who let Mom and Dad out of jail."

"Meg," Bass said sympathetically. "Your parents are serving life sentences. We did everything we could, but — "

"You *didn't* do everything you could!" the girl cried. "We found evidence that Frank Lindenauer worked for the terrorists! How come nobody figured that out, huh?"

Bass was stunned. "That's impossible!" Frank Lindenauer was the Falconers' CIA contact. By the time of the trial, he had flat-out vanished. How could two kids on the run have uncovered what a team of professional investigators had missed?

Aiden came back on the line. "We got into Lindenauer's old gym locker. He had a stack of flyers for a charity run by HORUS Global Group — and HORUS was a front for the terrorists."

"Remarkable!" exclaimed the attorney, making notes on a legal pad. "It could help the appeal. But you have to understand it doesn't prove anything to a judge. Just because Lindenauer may be guilty doesn't mean your parents are innocent."

"That's why we have to dig deeper," Aiden told him. "We need the information your firm gathered about HORUS."

Bass was bug-eyed. "For what?"

"To prove our parents were framed. We have to find Lindenauer. Someone from HORUS knows where he is."

"But there is no HORUS anymore," Bass

protested. "The FBI shut down their Denver head-quarters and all their satellite offices. Everybody associated with the group is in jail."

"Frank Lindenauer is out there somewhere," Aiden pointed out. "*He's* associated with HORUS. And there's a professional killer after us — "

Bass was more worried than ever. "A killer?"

"He might just be a big, bald psycho. Or maybe some yahoo who wants revenge on our parents. But what if he was hired by HORUS to tie up the loose ends?"

"All the more reason why you have to go to the police," Bass insisted. "You're in grave danger. Not just from this threat, but in general. Think of your mother and father. Surely it can't be your plan to add to their burdens."

Despite his powers of persuasion, Bass could not convince the Falconer siblings to give themselves up. They honestly believed that they were their parents' only chance for freedom. Bass swallowed a lump in his throat, torn between admiring their bravery and seeing nothing but tragedy in their future.

Their safety was his number one priority. But if they refused to be saved, he had to help them any way he could. With a heavy heart, he instructed Janine, his assistant, to fax the firm's file on HORUS Global Group to the number Aiden provided.

Janine sat unmoving in her swivel chair, the thick folder clutched to her chest. On the desk in front of her lay a copy of *The Washington Post*, open to page six. Her eyes were glued to Department of Juvenile Corrections photographs of Aiden and Margaret Falconer, and the headline above them:

$25,000 **REWARD OFFERED FOR CAPTURE**

OF FALCONER SIBLINGS

2

On the opposite side of the continent, a boy and a girl crouched in an alley in West Los Angeles, California. Although they were almost completely hidden behind an overloaded garbage Dumpster, the pair wore their LA Lakers caps tight and low, obscuring their faces.

There was a word for fugitives who took chances: "prisoners."

Aiden Falconer peered at the Staples superstore across the street. Somewhere in that building sat a sheaf of faxes from Mitchell Bass's law firm, hopefully untraced. Vital information about HORUS Global Group. The file was to be picked up by one Gary Graham.

Gary Graham — Aiden's alias.

He shuddered. The idea that an ordinary high school student should need an alias was pretty weird. Then again, nobody with the name Falconer could ever be considered ordinary.

Who would have believed that Mom and Dad would be in jail for treason? he thought glumly. *Or that Meg and I would be wanted by the FBI? Who would have believed that I'd be charged with arson, grand theft, breaking and entering, resisting arrest, and impersonating a police officer?*

Perhaps most bizarre of all was the fact that — except for the arson — those charges were true. Breaking the law was business as usual when you were on the run.

"Let's go," Meg urged. "It stinks here."

They waited for a break in the traffic and crossed to the Staples entrance. The store felt like a strange alternate universe. Every passing glance was a penetrating stare. Aiden held his breath and waited for the look of sudden recognition — the one that would be followed by shouts of: *It's those Falconer kids! Call the cops!*

His sister displayed no such trepidation. Classic Meg, cool under fire. Either that or she was too young and naive to realize that only the flimsiest onionskin layer of vigilance and pure luck separated them from disaster. They were almost famous now — "notorious" might be a better word. Every minute spent in public was a risk.

With a mixture of admiration and resentment,

Aiden watched her step brazenly up to the service desk. "I'm here to pick up a fax for Gary Graham."

To his amazement, the man behind the counter just gave it to her. Aiden was still fumbling for his fake ID when Meg thrust the file into his arms.

It was so unexpected that the precious documents slipped out of his hand and scattered to the floor. Urgently, the Falconers stooped to gather them up again.

That was when Aiden spotted the newspaper. *Why would somebody come into Staples to read the* LA Times?

All at once, a pair of eyes appeared above the headline. Alert, searching eyes.

Cop's eyes.

It's a setup!

3

The terror came in the form of a jolt of raw electricity. It shocked Aiden back to his feet, and he pulled his sister up with him by her fistful of crumpled faxes.

Their fugitive radar was so sensitive, their flight instinct so instant, that the Falconers were halfway to the exit before Aiden noticed two more sets of cops' eyes, attached to big bodies blocking the door.

All around the store, plainclothes officers were coming out of cover, advancing on the Falconers — one from the Stationery Department, one from Photo Processing, one from Computer Accessories —

We're trapped!

"What are we going to do?" hissed Meg in desperation.

Aiden had no answer. Staples had only one exit. If that was barred, there was no way out. Unless —

He made for Office Furniture, cramming the papers into his pockets as he ran. He selected a heavy steel computer desk that was on casters and swung it into the wide aisle.

Meg was bewildered. "What — ?"

There was no time for explanations. "The window," he ordered. "Fast!"

The fugitives got behind the desk and began wheeling it across the store, picking up speed as they headed for the plate glass storefront. Customers dove out of the way like tenpins as Aiden and Meg accelerated to a full sprint. The rollers sang against the terrazzo floor.

"Hey — stop!" One of the cops hurled himself into their path. He literally bounced off the flying desk, landing with a crash in a bin of ink-jet cartridges.

The other officers could only watch in frozen disbelief as the siblings blasted the desk into the floor-to-ceiling window.

Crash!

The glass shattered into a billion pieces and rained down all around them as they barreled into the street. The desk toppled and skidded across the sidewalk in a shower of sparks, slamming into a mailbox.

Aiden and Meg barely noticed the destruction. They were already half a block away, in full flight.

Six undercover LAPD officers burst out of the chaos of the store in hot pursuit.

It was a sensation that had become familiar in recent weeks — the searing chest-fire of a desperate high-stepping sprint. Yet this was no school track meet. The stakes were so high — escape or be arrested. Capture meant the end of all hope for Mom and Dad. That kind of urgency obliterated any discomfort. The pain was there, but the adrenaline of the moment overwhelmed everything.

Without missing a step, Aiden grabbed Meg's shoulder and steered her around the first corner. As they charged down the side street, Meg lurched to a sudden unscheduled stop in front of a boy and a girl who were walking in the opposite direction.

"Free hats!" she panted, taking her Lakers cap and placing it on the girl's head. "Support the home team!" She snatched Aiden's cap and tossed it to the boy. "Wear it with pride. Go, Lakers!" And the Falconers dashed off again.

Aiden risked a quick glance over his shoulder. No cops — not yet — just the bewildered boy and girl, sporting their new headgear. But the pursuers couldn't be far behind. The sound of distant sirens confirmed his worst fear. Word of their narrow escape had gone out over the police radio. Who knew how many officers the LAPD would send to bring in the fugitives who had converted the front of a Staples superstore into a heap of broken glass?

We'll never get away on foot!

"We need someplace to hide!" he rasped.

Meg looked around frantically. Identical three-story apartment buildings lined the block. "One of these doors must be unlocked — "

"No!" Aiden insisted. "The cops might go house-to-house!"

Then he saw it. A hundred yards ahead, where the street dead-ended at Olympic Boulevard, an enormous car transport came to a slow, grinding halt at the curb. The driver jumped out of the cab and disappeared inside a Burger King.

The Falconers didn't hesitate. They pounded down the road and across Olympic. Motorists swerved and slammed on the brakes. Horns sounded, and angry shouts rang out.

Aiden heard none of it. He was focused on the tractor trailer with such laser-straight singleness of purpose that the rest of the world barely existed. With Meg hot on his heels, he clambered up the steel grid of the double-decker rig's frame. The two hoisted themselves onto the top level and crawled inside a navy blue Honda Accord, shutting the doors behind them. Aiden stretched himself across the floor of the backseat; Meg snuggled into the space below the glove compartment.

"I can't believe we got away!" she rasped.

"Shhh — no talking. We're not away yet."

They cowered there, hardly daring to breathe, listening as police sirens converged on West Los Angeles. It was as mind-boggling as it was frightening. Being chased was nothing new. But never before had they been the targets of a massive manhunt by a big-city police force.

It's like something out of a movie, Aiden thought as squad cars raced past the tractor trailer where he and his sister lay hidden. *If somebody saw us — if they tell the cops —*

It was too awful to think about, all four Falconers in jail, no hope for the family.

Still, he could not keep his fevered brain from churning out worst-case scenarios. Even if they did somehow manage to evade this dragnet, then what? After today, LA would be hotter than a blast furnace. There would be no corner of this vast city where they could seek shelter, no rock large enough to hide under.

Yet leaving town would be even more perilous. Every bus depot, train station, and airport would be crawling with cops. There would be roadblocks, random searches, maybe even wanted posters.

His reverie was interrupted by the clang of heavy boots on the rig, followed by the slamming of a vehicle door.

A small moan of fright escaped Meg. If the police were going to search the cars on this transport, there would be no escape.

A split second later, the truck's motor started. Aiden ventured a peek out the Honda's window. It wasn't the cops. The driver had climbed behind the wheel of the cab and was seated there, drinking a tall soda through a straw. The tractor trailer roared to life, pulled out into traffic, and made a left turn.

Meg elevated herself just enough to peer out the passenger window. A dozen police cruisers dotted the street, sirens muted but lights still flashing. At the center of a sea of blue uniforms cowered the boy and girl from the side street, still wearing their newly acquired Lakers caps.

"Those poor kids," she whispered remorsefully.

"They'll be okay," Aiden shot back. "They're not us."

The transport slowed down as it picked its way between the parked squad cars.

It happened a split second before the driver was

able to speed up again. A Ford Taurus screeched up to the curb. The door was flung wide, and a very tall man unfolded himself and began lumbering across the road toward the center of activity.

Twin gasps escaped the Falconers, and they ducked back down again.

This was a man they knew all too well. He was Emmanuel Harris, the FBI agent who had arrested their parents and started this tragedy in motion. Now he was after them, never more than a few steps away — relentless and powerful.

The truck wheeled onto Santa Monica Boulevard, leaving Harris behind.

Aiden had a sinking feeling that they had not seen the last of him.

4

Take us away! Take us far away! The words echoed inside Meg's head as the car transport moved along the crowded freeway.

She peered outside, praying to see the open fields and countryside that would mean they had left Los Angeles. Instead, houses, houses, and more houses.

"Does this city ever end?" moaned Aiden from the backseat. It seemed as if they'd been driving forever and getting nowhere. How long had it been? An hour? More?

Time drags when you're scared out of your wits, Meg reflected.

The Honda's windows acted as a greenhouse for the relentless California sun. The car was an oven. Meg thought back to the news stories about babies and pets suffocating in hot, airless vehicles. It was all too easy to believe.

The rural scene she was hoping for never came. Instead, the neighborhoods grew more industrial —

rusty machinery, sprawling warehouses, high chain-link fences, some of them topped with razor wire.

The transport left the highway and began a laborious rumble over train tracks and broken pavement.

"Where *are* we?" Meg queried in frustration. "What kind of place is this?"

Aiden could only shake his head. After the wealth and polish of movie stars' homes and Hollywood glitz, their surroundings looked like something out of the *Terminator* movies.

Through the split in the Honda's front seat, brother and sister shared a look of dismay as the truck came to a stop in the middle of this alien landscape. Enormous cranes towered all around them, a titanic huddle of skyscraping robots, some with booms, some just steel skeletons, reaching for the stratosphere.

The motor died. They felt the vibrations as the driver stepped out and jumped to the ground.

"Now what?" whispered Meg.

They had thought only about escaping from Staples. Neither had any plan for what might come next.

Without warning, a dark shadow spread across the Honda's windshield, blocking the light.

Aiden and Meg cried out in shock and fear.

The shadow spread its wings and landed on the hood of the car. It stood there, staring in at them.

"A pelican!" Meg breathed. "Oh, man, I thought we were caught!"

"A pelican," Aiden repeated, weak with relief. "They're seabirds. We must be at the waterfront."

"This doesn't look like any beach I know," Meg said dubiously.

"Not a beach — a port. These cars are being shipped somewhere."

They permitted themselves a real look around. A vast commercial harbor stretched before them. The cranes were at the water's edge, loading and unloading an endless lineup of freighters, tankers, and barges at dozens of piers. The system of warehouses was a city on its own, teeming with dockworkers.

The place was ordered chaos, total activity, a beehive with sea breezes. Barely a square foot existed without a forklift on it, picking something up and putting it somewhere else. Almost as busy was the water itself, where tugs and service boats chugged around the bigger craft like mice swarming at the feet of an elephant.

Meg was dismayed. "How are we going to escape

from here? The minute we set foot on the dock, we'll stick out like sore thumbs! There isn't another kid for miles."

"We don't have to escape," Aiden told her evenly. "We're in a port. We're leaving here by boat."

Meg regarded him in awe. It made perfect sense. If they couldn't go by road, rail, or air, that left by sea. "You mean we just sit tight and get shipped out with these cars?"

"Of course not. This cargo could be going to Hong Kong. Fat lot of good we'd do Mom and Dad from over there."

She bristled. "If you've got a plan, spit it out. It's been a tough day."

"Listen — it's after seven. Chances are they won't unload this transport till morning. We wait for dark, find a ship that's heading up the coast somewhere, and stow away on it. As long as we don't leave the country, we should be okay to get where we need to go."

"Which is — ?" she prompted.

"Denver," he told her. "That's where HORUS had their head office."

"Mr. Bass said HORUS is history," his sister reminded him.

"Frank Lindenauer is still on the loose, and that means HORUS isn't dead. He can't be the only one who escaped."

"And you think the others are in Denver?" Meg asked.

"Maybe not, but that's where the trail starts."

It wasn't exactly a plan. But as long as there was a next step, a lead unexplored, it meant there was still hope.

"Okay," Meg agreed. "Denver."

The best thing about that city: It wasn't LA.

5

Aiden and Meg soon learned that full darkness never fell on the Port of Los Angeles. When the sun set, on came the floodlights, and the loading and unloading continued without interruption.

Meg was distraught. "What kind of workaholic port is this? Doesn't anybody go home?"

"They change shifts," Aiden guessed glumly. "It'll probably quiet down after midnight."

"After midnight? I'll die! I've already sweated a river. There's no air in here!"

"We'll crack the door a little. I'll take out the dome light first."

It helped with the heat but not the tension. Midnight approached, marking six hours that the Falconers had been stuck in the Honda.

Meg was restless to the point of insanity. "I've got to get out of here, bro!"

"Hang in there," Aiden urged.

Sure enough, on the stroke of twelve, longshoremen on the various projects began to drift away. A few job sites changed crews and continued working, but the majority of the floodlights were shut off.

It was an agonizing decision for Aiden: *Do we wait until the wharf is completely dark — which might never happen? Or do we risk it and go now?*

Meg was less conflicted. "Stay if you want, but I'm booking." And she was out of the Honda, climbing like a monkey down to the ground.

Aiden had no choice. He was right behind her. The clang of their sneakers against the metal frame of the car transport seemed like the ringing of a gong to them. In reality, it was all lost in the sounds of the harbor and the sea.

They dropped to the shadows underneath the rig.

"Stay out of the light," Aiden cautioned his sister. "I can pass for an adult in the dark, but no way you can. There must be security here. If they get a good look at you, they'll ask questions."

Meg bit her lip and did as she was told. This was no time for wounded pride.

They walked along the waterfront, steering clear of the brightly lit berths where the night crews were working.

While Meg hung back, Aiden ventured out onto the piers — there were thirty-two of them in this part of the harbor alone. Each ship was marked by a small sign that identified the vessel moored there, its port of origin, and its principal cargo. The information Aiden needed was at the bottom: destination and date and hour of departure.

The bigger the ship, the farther it seemed to be going — Tokyo, Seoul, Taipei, Manila. He targeted less impressive vessels, but even these seemed to be heading for South America. At last he focused on the smaller tramp freighters and bulk carriers.

San Diego — too close. It was almost a southern extension of Los Angeles. The cops down there probably cooperated with the LAPD. . . .

Alaska — too far . . . Vancouver — no good. They'd have to cross an international border to get back into the United States.

Perfect! The *Samantha D* was an independent freighter returning to its home port, Seattle, Washington. It was slated for loading at first light tomorrow, followed by a three P.M. departure. Cargo: 976 forty-two-gallon barrels of chili oil imported from Thailand.

Squinting into the gloom, Aiden checked out the ship as best he could. It looked big enough to hide in — half a football field long, and broad across the beam. There was a high structure in the bow — the conning tower? Aiden was no sailor, but he recalled some nautical terminology from books and movies. Astern, he could make out the silhouette of some kind of cargo-handling equipment. From this angle, he could see nothing amidships. He assumed that the opening to the hold was located there. Nine hundred seventy-six large barrels of chili oil would take up a lot of space. But he was sure there would be enough room for two fugitives trying to get out of LA.

The question is how to get on board without being seen.

The sound of laughing voices jolted him out of his thoughts. He ducked behind a cluster of wooden pylons and peered out furtively. Four sailors appeared from the darkness and strolled down the pier, singing raucously. They turned in at the *Samantha D* and clattered up the gangplank.

One of them said something about "taking the first watch," and Aiden felt a jolt of dismay. The full weight of what he and his sister were about to do came crashing down on him. All at once it occurred to him that they understood less than nothing about shipping. This boat could have a crew of five sailors or fifty. The Falconers had no idea what security measures might be in place. For all Aiden knew, the harbor police inspected every vessel, looking for stowaways. Where did he get off thinking they could pull a stunt like this with zero experience and zero planning?

The answer came as it had a dozen times since he and Meg had embarked on this insane adventure. They could do it because they *had* to. Because they owed it to their poor parents. Because there was no other way.

With that, Aiden Falconer, landlubber, set out to teach himself a very quick lesson in Stowaway 101.

He toyed with different possibilities, some of them unlikely, all of them bad — climbing up the mooring lines or scaling the hull from water level. As he weighed the options, Aiden suddenly remembered one of the main sources of his scant nautical knowledge. It came from a prison cell in Florida, more than three thousand miles away.

In addition to being a college professor of criminology, Dr. John Falconer was the author of a series of detective novels. In *Davy Jones's Locker*, the hard-boiled hero, Mac Mulvey, was investigating a ring of diamond smugglers in West Africa. In the exciting climax, Mulvey found the hot rocks by stowing away on a ship bound for New York City.

Aiden frowned. Dad's books were page-turners,

but the wild plotlines tended to blend together. How had Mulvey gained access to a working freighter full of smugglers?

Then he remembered — and wished he hadn't.

Mulvey hadn't snuck onto the boat at all. He'd had himself loaded aboard with the cargo.

6

"No way am I climbing into a barrel of chili oil!" Meg hissed in outrage.

"It wasn't chili oil in the story," Aiden tried to explain. "It was a shipload of handwoven carpets. He just rolled himself up in — "

"I don't care if it was a vat of sulfuric acid," his sister interrupted. "Mac Mulvey is a fictional character. What he does only works in books."

"Listen," Aiden reasoned. "We're not going to hide in real chili oil. We'll get into two empty barrels, and they'll load us up with the full ones. Yeah, it's risky. But not as risky as staying in LA."

Meg had to agree. Aiden's obsession with Dad's cheese-ball novels drove her nuts. But she couldn't deny that Mac Mulvey's far-fetched escape techniques had squeaked them through some very tough spots in the past.

According to the *Samantha D*'s documentation, its cargo was being housed in storage facility 13-Bravo, a single-story warehouse surrounded by a padlocked barbed-wire fence.

Through the smudged safety glass of the windows, the Falconers could see the steel drums, four to a pallet, lined up across the cement floor. Each was identified by a large green label: BANGKOK.

"That's it, all right," Meg confirmed. "Chili oil from Thailand."

"Yeah," said Aiden, looking worried. "But how are we going to get in?"

Wasn't that typical Aiden? Long on plans, short on execution. Wordlessly, she began to climb the chain-link fence, leading by example.

"But that's barbed wire!" her brother protested.

She swung a leg over the top, carefully avoiding the rusty barbs. "It's not rocket science, bro. If you don't touch them, they can't cut you." She jumped down to the ground. "See?"

If this hadn't been a matter of life and death for the Falconer family, Meg would have been laughing hysterically at the sight of her awkward, long-legged brother negotiating the fence. At the top, he was so terrified that his contortions actually put him in the way of the barbs. Pretty soon, he had one in his T-shirt and two in his jeans, and he was thrashing around, a fly caught in a spiderweb. Eventually, he worked his way loose but lost his hold on the fence in the process. He fell like a rock, landing in a heap beside his sister.

He quickly sprang back to his feet, huffing and daring her to comment. She didn't.

The warehouse door was also padlocked, but one of the windows had been propped open for ventilation. Aiden was able to get his shoulder under it and widen the gap with the strength of his upper body. In a couple of seconds, the agile Meg was over the ledge and in. With a good deal of grunting, Aiden managed to squeeze himself inside, too.

The two stood, breathing hard from the effort, staring at row after row of black shiny steel barrels. The drums were sealed, and yet the smell of oily hot peppers made their eyes water as if they were slicing onions.

"Wow," gasped Meg. "If this boat sinks, every fish in the Pacific is going to die of heartburn."

"Unless we collide with a tanker of Pepto-Bismol," Aiden agreed.

It sounded lighthearted, yet it was anything but.

A million things can go wrong with this plan, Meg reflected, *and none of them have to do with the boat sinking.*

Nine hundred seventy-six drums stood neatly in

place on pallets, ready for loading. But the Falconers were more interested in the empties that were stacked and sometimes strewn around the perimeter of the cargo. They selected one that was in good condition and dragged it over to the pallets.

That was where the problems started. A steel cask is heavy on its own. Fill it with forty-two gallons of dense chili oil, and you have an item that does not move easily. Both Falconers, pushing their hardest, could not budge a full barrel.

"This is impossible!" gasped Meg. "Let's get out of this place and find another way onto the ship."

It was just like Aiden to refuse to deviate from the plan. "This is the only way aboard," he insisted, grunting with effort. "We've got to make it work."

She sensed a note of rising panic behind his stubborn determination. "Yeah, but if we can't — "

And then, unexpectedly, the barrel moved. Not straight — instead, the drum spun on its circular base ever so slightly away from the other three.

Aiden frowned. "How did we just do that?"

Neither was exactly sure, but through trial and error they were able to wiggle the cask in alternating directions, "walking" it slowly toward the edge of the pallet.

Soon they were both drenched with sweat. It was

the most physically difficult thing Meg could ever remember doing. Every time they lost the twisting motion and tried to push the barrel in a straight line, progress would grind to a halt instantly. Yet after twenty minutes of backbreaking effort, the Falconers felt the heavy load begin to tip over the edge of the skid.

"Get clear!" Aiden warned. It came out as a papery rasp.

They both jumped back as the shiny black barrel hit the concrete floor with a teeth-jarring thud. It rolled a little, and both pounced on it, not wanting to waste its precious momentum. They kept it moving all the way to the wall and left it there among the empties. Aiden pulled off the Bangkok sticker and tax stamps and affixed them to the drum they had selected for themselves. Then he crouched down on the empty part of the pallet and tipped the open end of the cask over his head. He disappeared under it.

"How does it look?" came his muffled voice from inside.

Meg gawked. The warehouse was full of black barrels, and this was just another skid of four, exactly like the others. There was no way anyone would pick out Aiden's drum as different.

"Bro, you are one crazy genius! It's perfect! Is there room for both of us in there?"

The drum tipped up again, and Aiden struggled out. "Not unless we're mice. We'll have to free up another spot for you." He looked thoughtful. "Probably on a different skid."

She turned pale. "Just because we're in different barrels doesn't mean we can't go on the same pallet."

"Actually, it does. The full drums are a lot heavier than the empty ones. Even if we add in our weight, there's still going to be a big difference. If we're both on the same skid, somebody might notice that it's much lighter than the others."

She looked so unhappy that he chided, "Come on, Meg. It's not like we'll be passing notes between our barrels."

But they both knew the real reason for her unease. The horrible black cloud that had settled over the Falconer family held only a single thread of silver lining — the fact that Aiden and Meg had managed to stay together.

Separation, even by a few dozen feet in the same cargo, terrified them both.

7

The Ninth Precinct house of the Los Angeles Police Department was built into the side of a hill. It was a modern structure, with ceilings so low that six-foot-seven Emmanuel Harris had to duck in order to avoid whacking his head on the door frame of the office.

"Listen, Harris," the captain was saying. "We had eighty people on this. From precincts all over town. That's a ton of manpower." He shrugged. "The kids beat us."

The tall agent took a sip of coffee so rancid it may as well have bubbled straight out of the LA sewers. "Because you gave up," he accused.

"Because the citizens of this city look to us for protection, and I don't think two runaways pose much of a threat — even if their last name is Falconer."

"That's not the point," Harris insisted. "Those

two are in danger. I told you, there's a killer after them."

The captain was skeptical. "My men found no evidence of that."

"What evidence were you looking for — dead bodies?"

The captain drew himself up to his full height — still a foot shorter than his FBI visitor. "Maybe you think we all live in mansions and drive Porsches out here. This is a big town with big problems. We don't have unlimited funding like you feds. We have to pick our *priorities*."

Harris nodded sullenly. He knew the captain was right. Aiden and Margaret Falconer were news. If this kept up, they'd be almost as famous as their parents. But as a threat to public safety, they were pretty low on the totem pole.

"Tell me something," ventured the captain. "You made out like a bandit, taking down the parents — big promotion, your picture in the paper, American hero. Do you really have to arrest the whole family? Is it some kind of obsession with you?"

There was a lot Harris might have said to the LAPD man. Like: *Do you know how it feels to lie awake nights, wondering if you put the wrong people in prison? That their innocent children are desperate fugitives, thanks to you?*

In the course of their weeks on the run, Aiden and Margaret had managed to unearth bits of evidence about the mysterious Frank Lindenauer — the missing piece of their parents' story. It wasn't enough to overturn two life sentences. But an FBI agent survived on hunches. Harris had an awful hunch there was more to this Lindenauer thing than met the eye.

The case was closed, the traitors behind bars. If Harris didn't go after the truth, no one else would.

That was his "obsession" with the Falconers — not to harm them, but to help them.

He had shattered this family. Now he was their only hope.

The loading of the freighter *Samantha D* began promptly at six o'clock the next morning.

Crouched inside the upended barrel, Aiden listened to the clatter of the loading bay door rolling open. Next came the roar of the forklifts. Like worker ants, they picked up the cargo one skid at a time and delivered it to the wharf.

When Aiden felt the jolt of the lift mechanism

take hold of the pallet beneath his feet, he nearly jumped out of his skin. It was terrible enough to be facing the loading procedure, knowing that discovery and arrest could happen at any minute. But to do so in blind helplessness, never knowing what was coming or when, was sheer agony.

Even worse was the thought that, a few pallets away, on another forklift, his little sister had to go through this torture.

Will she have the mental toughness to handle it?

His one comfort was the fact that eleven-year-old Meg had more toughness in her pinky toe than he would ever have in his entire body.

His barrel rattled as the forklift jounced over the uneven tarmac. Desperately, he braced his arms against the sides and tried to push down. The drums were not fastened. They were supposed to be anchored by the weight of their contents. If the bumpy ride knocked over his hiding place, there he'd be, hunkered over on his skid, trying to pass for forty-two gallons of chili oil. It was a mind-numbing thought. He could only hope that Meg knew enough to try to keep her barrel in place.

All at once, the motion stopped, and a large bump told him that his skid had been set down. He could hear the jokes and small talk of the dockworkers just inches away, and he held his breath and prayed.

Is this it? Am I on the boat?

Suddenly, the skid shot up into the sky as if propelled by a jet pack. It soared and rocked as the crane lifted it high over the Port of Los Angeles. When Aiden dared to open his eyes, a horrifying sight greeted them. Light was coming in from below. Through the framework of wooden slats, he could make out small figures on the dock.

And if I can see them, they can see me!

He hung there, clinging to the walls of the drum, willing the dockworkers not to look up. Amazingly, none did. The skid swung in a wide arc out over the pier and the *Samantha D* and was lowered at dizzying speed into a darkened place.

Heart nearly jumping out of his chest, Aiden realized that he was on board in the ship's cargo hold. Now all he had to do was wait — and pray for Meg.

Meg crouched in the black prison of the barrel, listening to the thrum of the ship's engine and the lapping of the sea against the hull.

The *Samantha D* had been under way for about an hour, she guessed, but that didn't mean it was safe to come out. There had been crew members working in the hold up until a few minutes ago, securing the cargo. Now, at last, the coast seemed to be clear.

She and Aiden had talked a lot about stowing away but not at all about what to do once they'd made it this far.

Aiden. Had he made it aboard? Was he coming out of his barrel right now to look for her? She had to believe it because the alternative was just too awful to contemplate.

She needed to see his face, to throw her arms around him and hold him tight. And when she was through hugging him, she was going to punch his stupid head in! The next time he got a half-baked idea to follow in Mac Mulvey's footsteps, he could count her *out*!

She would never forgive him for the misery, discomfort, and sheer terror of being loaded onto the *Samantha D*. When that crane had yanked her halfway to the moon, leaving her stomach on the ground —

Let it go, she soothed herself. *It's over. Time to get out from under this thing and find your brother.*

She leaned against the back of the cask to raise the front. It would not budge.

The explosion of panic nearly took her consciousness. *The barrel's heavy, but not that heavy! Up on the crane, it took all my strength to keep it from falling off!*

She tried again, but there was no movement. It was as if the steel had been melded to the pallet beneath her feet.

She felt the round walls of the drum closing in on her. She was trapped, stuck in here all the way to Seattle! How many days was that? She had no food, no water! She would have to pound on the side of the barrel and scream for the crew to rescue her! She wouldn't die, but she'd be caught.

She lowered her shoulder and rammed it into the steel with all her strength. Nothing. Not even a hiccup.

How is that possible?

8

Sixty feet to her left, on the opposite side of the cargo hold, a drum shifted, then tilted. Two eyes looked furtively out, sweeping the semi-dark area for sailors. Satisfied there were none, Aiden squeezed himself out of the cask, careful to set it back down quietly on its skid.

He massaged the cramped muscles in his legs, apprehensive and a little disappointed. Knowing his impulsive sister, he'd half expected to find her already tapping on barrels and demanding to know if he intended to stay in there all night.

I'd better go find her.

He stepped off the skid — and fell five feet straight down to the steel deck of the hold. He was more shocked than hurt. Looking up, he realized what had just happened to him. The skids had been double stacked. He had just walked off the upper level.

Look on the bright side, he told himself. *It's a good*

thing my skid didn't end up on the bottom row, under a ton of chili oil.

All at once, he realized, or thought he did, why Meg had not been waiting to greet him when he emerged from his cocoon. She was under there somewhere, trapped. And, God help him, he wasn't even sure he could get her out.

It took an hour just to find her. He didn't dare make any noise, so his options were reduced to going from skid to skid, barrel to barrel, tapping lightly, searching for the drum that would tap back.

Poor Meg was so terrified that she didn't even dare reply for fear the tapper was not her brother. It was the hollow sound that told Aiden he had found the right one.

"Meg!" he whispered. "Is that you?"

"Aiden!" came her muffled voice. "I can't get out! The barrel won't move!"

"I know," he told her. "There's another skid piled on top of you."

There was a pause, then, "I guess Mac Mulvey never thought of that."

Aiden was almost grateful for the jab. It meant that Meg was still Meg.

"Listen, I'm going to try to push the barrel off the skid. But you'll have to help me, okay?"

He heard fear in her voice. "I don't know which way to push. It's pitch-black in here, Aiden! It's like being in a coffin!"

"Just follow my lead," he soothed. "When you feel the barrel moving, heave along with me."

At first it was like trying to move a building off its foundation. Aiden's muscles were stiff from twelve hours of crouching in a drum. He was weak from lack of food and water and exhausted from lack of sleep.

He tried to "walk" the drum forward, the way he and Meg had moved the full ones in the warehouse. But the weight from above made that impossible.

He threw his head back to howl his frustration to the world and caught himself just in time, almost choking on the sound he must not make. Stark terror flooded over him. He had very nearly brought the entire crew belowdecks to investigate. With the panic came the adrenaline, and that lent him hidden reserves of strength. The barrel began to slide. A few seconds later, he was slumped across it, completely spent. But the mouth of the drum had moved halfway off the skid.

Meg was thin and lithe, but she would never know a tighter squeeze. There was a six-inch gap between the pallet and the deck. Her feet and legs came through first, and that was pretty painless. Her upper body was tougher going. It took Aiden, yanking on her legs with all his might, to force her head through that tiny space. Her cheek was scraped raw and bleeding. Tears streamed down her face, but she uttered not one whimper.

In the real world, they would have rushed to the nearest hospital for first aid. Here, Meg just dried her eyes and mopped up the blood with the hem of her T-shirt. They managed to jam the barrel back into place.

Having escaped from the cargo, they burrowed right back into it. The drums were lined up with almost military precision, but there were still openings between the pallets where a body could lie in hiding. Both had to position themselves on their sides, curled around a barrel.

"I hope you remember the way out of here," Meg murmured. "I didn't go through all this to be lost in a maze of stink oil."

"It won't be forever," Aiden promised.

Meg nodded, exhausted. "How long does it take to get to Seattle?"

"The sign on the pier gave an ETA of noon Thursday. That's a little less than two days. But there's no way we can stay down here that long."

She looked at him dubiously. "Why not? Have we been invited to movie night with the crew?"

"For food," he told her, growing annoyed with her sarcasm. "We haven't eaten in a day and a half. We'll never make it to Seattle unless we get some sustenance — at least some water."

"I'm starving," she agreed. "But we can't just raid the kitchen like this is sleepaway camp."

"I've already thought of that," said her brother. "A ship has to have lifeboats. That's the law. And shouldn't lifeboats be stocked with food and water?"

She eyed him with suspicion. "Did you think of that, or did it come from Dad's book?"

"That one came from me," Aiden swore. "I mean, it's only reasonable, right? What would you put in a lifeboat — bricks?"

"I'd put Frank Lindenauer," Meg said readily. "And a tape recorder. And as soon as he admitted how he framed Mom and Dad, I'd set the boat on fire."

Aiden sighed. Here in the forest of chili oil, Frank Lindenauer seemed as remote as the planet Pluto. Sure, Aiden realized that bringing in the traitor was their ultimate purpose. But there were so many steps between the cargo hold of the *Samantha D* and that goal — making it to Seattle; sneaking ashore; finding a way to Denver; picking up the trail of HORUS Global; and hoping that it led to Lindenauer. Throw Agent Harris into the mix — he certainly wasn't going to back off. And Hairless Joe, the mysterious bald assassin who had followed them across three thousand miles —

One day at a time, he thought. *One hour at a time.* In the past weeks, it had often come down to minute by minute, second by second.

Midnight in the hold. Only deep space could be darker.

The Falconers had tried to get some sleep while waiting for their chance to sneak out to the lifeboat. But Meg had found her eyes simply wouldn't close. One reason was the uncomfortable position of lying on a hard wooden pallet, squeezed between steel barrels. The hunger pangs and parching thirst didn't help, either. Most of all, Aiden and Meg were both too keyed up to relax.

At last they worked their way out of the cargo. Meg was amazed at how much she could suddenly see. A three-quarter moon barely showed through the thick cloud cover, but hours in the black velvet labyrinth of drums had boosted their night vision.

The only way out of the hold was a metal ladder built into the bulkhead. They climbed with extreme caution, Aiden in the lead. He peered out over the main deck.

Meg held her breath, waiting for her brother's report. If the coast wasn't clear now, with the majority of the crew in their bunks, then it never would be.

Aiden ducked back down. "I don't see anybody on deck," he whispered. "But there must be a team on the bridge."

"Will they spot us?" Meg asked nervously.

"Not if they're keeping their eyes on the road," was Aiden's reply. "But maybe we should wait — "

"No chance," Meg interrupted. "We go now, before we can talk ourselves out of it."

Two twelve-foot-long lifeboats hung above the gunwale on either side of the ship, just forward of the hold. The starboard one was closer. Aiden and Meg heaved themselves on deck and scampered through the dark shadows.

Meg got there first. She climbed up on the rail, threw open the covering tarpaulin, and slipped beneath it. Then she reached down a hand and helped Aiden in beside her. The entire operation, so much dreaded, was over in seconds.

They crouched there for a long moment, waiting to hear the outcry of "Intruders on board!" It didn't come.

"We made it," Aiden breathed.

Meg nodded. "Now let's eat."

The lifeboat's provisions were sealed in a large waterproof duffel in the prow. The half-starved Falconers tore eagerly through the plastic shell, coming up with the bottled water first. They drank greedily. It was warm, and twenty-four hours of breathing chili oil fumes gave everything an odd, spicy taste. But to Aiden and Meg, it had just bubbled straight out of the purest spring at the North Pole. Nothing had ever been so refreshing.

They turned their attention to the food next. There were a lot of energy bars and high-protein snacks like nuts and raisins. Large shrink-wrapped packages contained prepared meals to serve ten — beef Stroganoff, mac and cheese, chili con carne, and chicken goulash.

Aiden held up a compact aluminum saucepan with a foldout handle. "There's a Sterno stove, too," he whispered. "And matches. I think you put these pouches in boiling water."

"Let's not and say we did," grinned Meg, ripping into the Stroganoff.

The Falconers dug into the cold, salty feast, using plastic spoons to savor every bite of unheated meat and congealed gravy. For dessert, they stuffed themselves with M&M trail mix and washed it down with more bottled water.

Aiden leaned back with a contented sigh and patted his stomach. "Remember Thanksgiving dinner?"

Meg emitted the kind of rolling burp that was considered a great compliment in many world cultures. "Dad's roast turkey. Mom's mashed potatoes. Pumpkin pie — "

"Well, this was better," he said positively. "Not more fun. Just better."

"We never appreciated those times," Meg commented. "The two of us fought through every course of those dinners."

"Who knew that your whole life could be taken away with the bang of a judge's gavel?"

They lapsed into a melancholy silence, broken eventually by Meg's yawn. "You never did tell me how Mac Mulvey survived on that ship all the way from Africa."

"Don't ask," Aiden replied, his words slurred. The forces of fatigue acting on the brother and sister were all coming together — sleeplessness, a place to lie down, and suddenly-full stomachs after a long fast.

The onset of drowsiness was so unexpected, so overwhelming, that neither could even think to fight it.

"You wouldn't believe it anyway . . ." Aiden tried to continue.

By the time the mumbled sentence trailed off, both Falconers had fallen into a deep, dreamless slumber.

The side of the hanging lifeboat lurched, tossing Meg up against her brother. Their heads connected with a sharp *thwack*, and they both came awake with a start.

"What the — ?"

Aiden clamped a hand over his sister's mouth.

Full daylight streamed in through the draped edges of the tarp. They had slept all the way through the remainder of the night. Now they were trapped in this lifeboat, suspended above the deck of a busy working ship.

But why are we bouncing around like Ping-Pong balls?

The answer came in the form of a gust of wind that plucked at the tarp covering them. Stealthily, Aiden peeked out of the canvas on the ocean side. Whitecaps were everywhere, reaching up for the lowering sky. The *Samantha D* bucked like a bronco, riding the breaking swells. A cascade of spray hit Aiden in the face. He dropped the tarp and backed away from the edge.

"What's going on?" Meg demanded.

"Rough seas," Aiden whispered. "It probably feels worse to us because this lifeboat's hanging on pulleys."

She was alarmed. "Let's get out of here!"

"Shhhh! We can't. There are sailors all over the deck." She looked terrified, so he added, "It's not the end of the world. We can hide here as easily as in the hold. We just can't make any noise — and that means *none*."

The boat heaved again, and she groaned. "I can't stay here — I get seasick!"

Aiden, who had known her all her life, looked dubious. "Since when?"

"Since the fifth-grade boat trip on the Chesapeake. I was the only kid who barfed."

"Why didn't you tell me that while we were still on dry land?" he demanded.

"Would it have made any difference?" she hissed back. "This was the only way out of LA."

"Listen," said Aiden. "The minute it gets dark, we'll sneak back to the hold. Meanwhile, hang on tight. And try not to throw up. Somebody might notice the smell. There's a first aid kit in here. I'll see if there's anything for motion sickness."

The kit had no seasickness remedy. It did, however, contain an antibiotic cream, which he applied to the scrapes and cuts on his sister's face.

As the ship pitched and tossed, they settled in to do battle with landlubbers' nausea — knowing all the while that a little queasiness was the least of their worries.

The crash came just after thirteen hundred hours. It was followed by a random clatter, all coming from the hold.

Seaman Emilio Lopez was the first down the ladder, noting with some relief that the cargo seemed well battened down. So what was the noise that sounded like a bull had gotten loose in a china shop?

The clatter came again, and Lopez ducked his head just in time. A loose barrel came flying through the air, missing him by inches. Lithe and quick, he cornered it against a bulkhead and held it there, shouting for assistance.

Crewmen came climbing down into the hold and helped secure the wayward drum.

First Mate Rod Bergeron was the last one on the scene. His observation cut right to the heart of the matter: "Why is that barrel empty?"

They searched the hold but could not find the missing lid or any spilled chili oil.

"Take a stick and tap on all these barrels," Bergeron instructed. "Make sure we don't have any other empties. I'm going up to the comm room."

"What is it, Mr. B?" asked Lopez.

"Probably just a cargo snafu," the first mate replied. "But I'm going to radio the company. See if anything of ours got left behind."

Twenty minutes later, Bergeron was in the conning tower, talking on ship-to-shore with the manager of storage facility 13-Bravo in the Port of Los Angeles. Sure enough, his crew had located two full drums of chili oil, labels removed, among the empties.

"*Two* drums?" Bergeron repeated. He reached for a walkie-talkie. "Mr. Lopez, we think there might be another dummy down there."

"Just found it, Mr. B. Same as the first — empty, with no lid. We're looking for more."

Bergeron thought it over. "Belay that search, and start a new one."

The crewman's voice was confused. "Mr. B?"

"I want this ship torn apart rivet by rivet," the first mate ordered. "I think we might have a couple of hitchhikers."

* * *

By two o'clock that afternoon, the sea had grown no calmer. The pitch and roll of the *Samantha D*'s starboard lifeboat had settled into a stomach-churning carnival ride.

If anything, Aiden was even more seasick than Meg. *I feel like I'm going to die, and I'm afraid I won't,* he reflected, struggling to keep his spirits up and his lunch down.

Meg turned over listlessly and checked her brother's watch for at least the thirtieth time. "Two-forty-nine," she reported. "Nine hours and eleven minutes till midnight." Midnight was when they'd agreed it would be safe to sneak back to their hiding place amid the cargo drums in the hold.

"I can't promise it'll be much better down there," Aiden cautioned her. "When the sea is rough, it counts for the whole ship."

"Yeah, but at least we won't be swinging," she groaned. "I mean, what could be worse than this?"

The words were barely out of her mouth when a loud, repeating Klaxon cut the air and an amplified voice crackled, *"All hands on deck. All hands."*

The Falconers lay frozen with shock. What was going on?

"We've got to get out of here!" Meg whispered urgently. "We're sinking!"

Aiden was no calmer, but at least he was logical. "If we're sinking, we're in exactly the right place. But they didn't say 'abandon ship.'" He raised the tarpaulin and peered through the gap.

The deck below the conning tower swarmed with sailors in shiny yellow rain gear. A man who appeared to be in charge barked a few orders, and the crew scattered.

Aiden squinted to get a better view through the driving downpour. "What are they doing?" he mumbled aloud. From his pocket, he pulled out a dainty pair of mother-of-pearl opera glasses that had once belonged to none other than Frank Lindenauer. Aiden had first taken them as a possible clue to the traitor's whereabouts. But they came in handy as mini-binoculars, too.

Now he trained them on the crew of the *Samantha D*, hoping to discover their purpose, fearing that he already knew it.

"They're abandoning ship, right?" Meg demanded.

"Worse." Aiden watched a moment longer. The sailors were opening hatches, peering down companionways, riffling through equipment bins. "They're searching. For us."

Meg went rigid with fear. "But how did they find out we're on board?"

"It doesn't matter how they found out. They know. And this lifeboat is one of the first places they'll check." He reached under the duffel of supplies and pulled out two rain ponchos.

She gawked. "We're about to get caught, and you're worried about a little *rain*?"

"The whole crew's wearing yellow slickers just like these," he explained rapidly. "In this visibility, they're not going to see faces; they'll just see another couple of raincoats walking by."

"Yeah, but walking to *where*?"

"To where they've already searched. That's the safest place right now." He fitted the poncho over her head and put his own on. "Quick — before they work their way around to this side."

They jumped down to the heaving deck, which was slick with rain and spray. Of all the wild schemes they'd hatched over these weeks on the run, this seemed the most foolhardy — *to march directly through the ranks of the very people who are looking for you.*

Yet it seemed to be working! They brushed right behind two sailors who were rummaging through an equipment locker, and they scooted straight through the center of activity on the main deck. The crew was so concerned with investigating every nook and cranny that they had no eyes for two figures in plain sight.

The deck lurched, and Aiden nearly lost his footing. Meg caught his arm and steadied him, even as she tried to stand taller in her squall gear.

This whole illusion disappears the instant we attract attention, Aiden reminded himself. *And then we're dead.*

He looked around, panic-stricken. Yellow slickers were everywhere. There was no place that seemed free of them, no safe haven beckoning. Except —

The steel conning tower loomed over them against the rain-streaked sky. Had it been searched yet? It was impossible to know. But another argument tugged at him: All hands on deck meant a minimum crew on the bridge — maybe even just one sailor at the wheel.

He hustled Meg ahead of him through the hatch to the ship's main superstructure. The place reminded Aiden of the inside of a submarine the family had once visited at a naval museum — cramped space, low ceiling, and everything battleship gray. It was deserted — their gamble had paid off. But the clatter of heavy footsteps on metal surfaces rang all around them. They had to disappear, and right now.

Companionways led in several different directions, but Aiden's eyes fell on the hatch marked TANK ACCESS.

His heart quickened. If that meant what he thought it did, they had found a hiding place where no one would ever think to look for them.

A narrow ladder led up a claustrophobic tube that rose a full forty steps into the guts of the tower. At the top, a domed surface appeared before them, stretching ten feet across and made of heavy-grade reinforced steel.

Meg was mystified. "The gas tank?"

Aiden shook his head. "Water. An oceangoing vessel has to carry its own fresh water." He reached out onto the gently rounded surface to the circular rubber-sealed hatch in front of him. The hatch-lock wheel was well oiled and turned easily. Aiden threw open the cover and looked down.

About five feet of water sloshed with the motion of the ship in a tank that was seven feet deep — enough to meet the drinking, cooking, and bathing needs of a crew of twenty-eight on a short voyage. Ladder rungs, similar to those in the hold, ran down the curve of the wall to the bottom.

Gritting his teeth, Aiden swung himself over the

edge and climbed down into the tank. The water felt clammy as his jeans soaked it up and like slush as it filled his shoes.

He shuffled over on the rungs, making room for his sister. She grimaced as her lower body was submerged.

"Aw, man, this is nasty!" was her whispered complaint.

Soon they were both hanging on to the top rung, their heads and shoulders above water level, the rest of them under. Aiden reached up and pulled the hatch closed over them.

The darkness was suffocating.

Meg took a slosh in the face. "This is *him*, isn't it?" she sputtered accusingly. "Mac Mulvey — this is how *he* stowed away."

"I know it's awful," Aiden admitted, "but they'll never find us here."

It was the one argument that put an end to all others. Comfort was nice, but freedom was mandatory. It was the only way to keep hope alive for Mom and Dad.

Whatever it took.

11

Aiden and Meg had known many hardships since their escape from Sunnydale Farm in Nebraska. But never had they suffered such exquisite torture as they now experienced in the water tank of the *Samantha D*.

It might have been day; it might have been night. It might have lasted a minute, an hour, a week. The Falconers hung there in abject misery, deprived of all sensation save the ache in their arms and the chill in their bones.

The water had seemed cold to Meg at first contact. Now, a few hours later, she might as well have been standing with a family of penguins in Antarctica.

"I can't feel my feet," she said plaintively. In the crushing silence of the tank, her words were echoing bomb blasts.

Aiden's teeth were chattering. "I know. I'm freezing, too."

"No," she insisted, her voice growing shrill. "I honestly can't feel them. Like my legs fade out at the knees."

"Shhh," he soothed, reaching out his own leg to try to massage some life back into hers. "You're fine, Meg. I think you lost a shoe, but that's it."

She was relieved, embarrassed, and terrified at the same time. "I'm starting to go nuts, Aiden. There's no way I can last all the way to Seattle in here."

She had never before heard defeat in her own voice, and that distressed her more than this horrible tank or the angry sea outside.

He drew her into his arms, and they clung together. There was no body heat left for them to share, but at least they could feed off each other's strength.

Captain McNicholl ran the *Samantha D* with a no-nonsense style and expected the same from the officers under his command.

"Well, are they on the ship or aren't they?"

"Definitely aboard, skipper," Bergeron told him. "They were into the provisions in the starboard lifeboat. But darned if we can find them."

The captain frowned. "They can't be illegal aliens — they were already in the country when they boarded. Who would hop a domestic freighter?"

The first mate shrugged. "Thrill seekers?"

McNicholl didn't buy it. "We do twenty knots with a tailwind. You'd find more thrills on a city bus."

The ship's cook, Frenchie, stepped up the companionway to the bridge. The only thing French about him was his name, Al French. But the crew of the *Samantha D* liked to be able to say that their meals were prepared by a French chef. "Got a minute, Captain?"

"Not now, Frenchie."

"You'll want to hear this," the cook insisted. "The water's down to a trickle in the galley — "

"This isn't the time for another one of your plumbing stories," Bergeron said impatiently.

"So I opened up the main pipe," Frenchie went on, "and pulled out *this*." He held up a waterlogged Keds sneaker, size four.

McNicholl and Bergeron exchanged a look of pure shock. "The water tank!"

Thirty seconds later, they were climbing the narrow ladder in the access tube. Bergeron threw the hatch cover wide, and the captain and first mate stared in naked disbelief down into the opening.

Two shivering kids clung together in the churning water. Their lips were blue, their faces chalk white.

Like most places aboard the *Samantha D*, the storage compartment was cramped and uncomfortable. It was doubly so for Aiden and Meg, who huddled in thick blankets in the gloomy clutter. The only light came from a small porthole that peeked out just a few inches above deck level. With the worsening weather and the onset of night, soon they were in total darkness. Although the air was stuffy, they felt as if they'd never be warm again.

All this was minor compared with the reality of what had happened.

"I guess this proves that even the great Mac Mulvey isn't perfect," Meg mumbled in a hollow tone.

Aiden shook his head miserably. "I can't believe they caught us. It's crazy — I mean, we always knew this plan was a long shot. But — "

Meg nodded. "We beat the odds so many times, we figured we could keep on doing it."

"We were stupid. Everybody runs out of miracles sooner or later."

"Not necessarily," his sister said hopefully. "Maybe the crew won't figure out who we are."

There was a click as the hatch was unlocked. A

blinding beam shone in their faces. They shielded their eyes from the sudden painful light.

"So," came the unpleasant voice of Rod Bergeron, "how does it feel to be the children of *traitors*?"

The chill of the water tank was suddenly toasty compared with the liquid nitrogen that flooded Aiden's gut. What was worse than being found? Being found out.

"I don't know what you're talking about."

"Don't play me," the sailor snarled. "How many fugitives are your age, and running from LA? You made quite an impression back there. They had half the police force out looking for you. It'll be a big family reunion for you and your rotten parents — behind bars."

Aiden bit his lip, but Meg was not as restrained. "Our parents are more patriotic than you'll ever be!"

Bergeron's scowl got even uglier. "You're talking to someone who wore the uniform of this country! Who saw action in the First Gulf War! Anybody lucky enough to be born here who betrays America should be strung up, and their delinquent kids with them!"

"You'll eat those words when we prove they're innocent!" Meg raged.

But her promise was empty, and both Falconers

knew it. The quest to exonerate their parents had come to an abrupt end. It was another juvenile detention facility for Aiden and Meg — one with bars instead of barns this time.

The first mate tossed their dried clothes and an oversize Ziploc bag down on a coil of heavy mooring line. That clear pouch contained all their possessions in the world, in varying degrees of water damage. The opera glasses seemed unhurt, but the faxes from Staples were little more than pulp. There was also a leaflet from a charity connected to HORUS Global. It had fared slightly better — faded, but still readable. Most important was Aiden's nine-year-old vacation snapshot of "Uncle Frank" himself — their first, and still their best, clue in the search for the man who had framed their parents. It was crinkled and soggy, but the image was intact.

Missing from the collection was about eighty dollars. Aiden could only assume it had been stolen, probably by Bergeron himself. He found it very hard to worry about a little money at this awful moment, with the future of the Falconer family evaporating before their eyes.

Besides, he reminded himself, *more than half the cash was counterfeit, anyway.* That phony fifty was a souvenir of their brief association with an LA street gang.

The first mate sneered at the Ziploc. "The famous Falconers, mucking around the cargo, bribing the rats with a bagful of junk. Is that what your parents sold out their country for? You disgust me!"

For a moment, Aiden thought he might actually spit at them. Instead, Bergeron set the flashlight down on the coil of rope. "The captain says to leave you this. He doesn't want the baby terrorists to be afraid of the dark." He stepped out of the compartment and then wheeled to face them once more. "You'll be happy to know that the FBI was very interested to learn we've got you on board. They're sending an agent to meet you at the dock in Seattle. An old friend of yours, they say. Guy named Harris."

The hatch slammed shut. They heard the key turn.

"J. Edgar Giraffe," Meg groaned, using their nickname for the six-foot-seven Emmanuel Harris. "Why does it have to be him?"

"Doesn't matter," Aiden said glumly. "Caught is caught."

After unfolding a tarpaulin to use as a privacy

curtain, they got dressed. Their meager possessions, lightened by theft, disappeared easily into their pockets. Most of the fax was ruined, but Meg saved the pages that were still readable.

We'll be trading it all for Juvie jumpsuits tomorrow, Aiden reflected despondently.

As he crumpled up the spoiled papers, he frowned at the rectangular object he and Meg were using as a makeshift table. It resembled a suitcase except for its color — nobody made luggage in fluorescent orange, did they?

Then his eyes fell on the plastic packaging: PORTABLE LIFE RAFT — PULL TAB TO INFLATE.

Meg read it, too, her jaw setting into a profile of grim determination. "We are so out of here, bro!"

Aiden stared at her. "What — in this?"

"It's a boat."

"It's a rubber raft," he amended. "That's open ocean out there — in the middle of a storm!"

"If you've got a better plan, let's hear it," Meg challenged. "In fourteen hours we chug into Seattle, where J. Edgar Giraffe will be waiting on the dock."

Aiden swallowed hard. Neither of them knew anything about sailing or navigation. And here they were, ready to take on a full gale in a souped-up kiddie pool. It was so typical of his sister: impractical, impossible, crazy — and yet totally *necessary*. Once in FBI custody, their chance of escape would dwindle to absolute zero. They had to get away *now*.

"You're right," he told her. "But in case you haven't noticed, we're in a locked storeroom. We've got to get out of *here* before we can use the life raft."

She favored him with a slight grin. Good old Meg — no spot was ever so tight that she couldn't come up with a smile. He both loved and hated that about her.

"Bro," she said, "that's the easy part."

He grimaced. Compared to what lay ahead, almost anything would be the easy part.

12

Seaman Lopez stepped gingerly down the companionway to the storage compartment where the stowaways were being held. It took all his sea legs to keep from spilling the dinner tray Frenchie had prepared for the two young prisoners. The deck twisted and bucked beneath his feet. Even for an experienced sailor, this was an awful night to be aboard ship.

Balancing the tray on one hand — quite a feat in these seas — he fiddled for the key, unlocked the hatch, and stepped inside. This whole affair made him uneasy. The *Samantha D* was a freighter, not a prison barge. Arrests at sea, holding cells, captives — they were just kids, for heaven's sake!

The tarpaulin came out of nowhere, straight down over his head. Suddenly, he was lost in what seemed like acres of fabric. "Hey — "

"Now!" Meg cried.

Aiden stretched out a foot and tripped the figure

under the canvas. Lopez went down in a mess of up-ended chicken and mashed potatoes. Meg was on top of him like a shot, wrapping flailing arms and legs with duct tape. Aiden joined the fray, pressing his full weight down on the struggling sailor.

"Nothing personal, mister," grunted Meg, tying her quarry up tight. "We're actually nice people, but we've got to get out of here."

"But where can you go?" the sailor's muffled voice protested.

"Trust me," Aiden said feelingly, "you don't want to know."

Lopez read their intentions from the dread in Aiden's voice. *"Overboard?"* He stopped fighting. "In these conditions? You don't have a prayer!"

"We don't have a prayer if the FBI gets us," Meg snapped.

"Don't do it!" Lopez pleaded, thrashing again. "You'll drown!"

Aiden and Meg piled heavy coils of rope onto the tarpaulin, pinning Lopez to the deck.

"You seem like a good guy," Meg told him. "Thanks for caring about us. Nobody else does." Then she turned to Aiden and said, "Showtime."

Aiden snatched the handle of the portable life raft — and very nearly yanked his arm out of its socket.

He peered down at the label: NET WEIGHT: 32 KG/ 70.4 POUNDS.

"Meg — give me a hand!"

Together, they managed to drag the heavy valise out the hatch and up the companionway.

"What have they got in here?" Meg panted. "Anvils?"

The *Samantha D* was pitching so violently that they had to get on all fours and push the life raft across the deck to the gunwale. Luckily, the night was near black, with terrible visibility through the driving rain.

Easier to trip over us than spot us in these conditions, Aiden thought.

"Here goes nothing." He grasped the inflation tab and pulled.

There was a crack, followed by the loud hiss of compressed gas. The valise seemed to erupt, swelling and unfolding like time-release photography of a flower coming to bloom. In seconds, the suitcase shape was gone, replaced by a circular raft eight feet in diameter, enclosed by a canopy. Inside, the craft was fully stocked with life jackets, paddles, signal flares, food, water, and a first aid kit.

They gawked. It was tough to feel anything beyond raw fear at a moment like this. But both couldn't help but be impressed by such a marvel of engineering.

And then they were captured in a flashlight beam.

"Freeze!" roared the furious voice of Rod Bergeron.

The command had the exact opposite effect. Aiden and Meg burrowed themselves under the rubberized base and pushed with all their might. The big life raft rose up and toppled over the rail, plummeting to the turbulent waves below. Propelled by an explosive mix of panic and purpose, Aiden and Meg scrambled after it, hurling themselves clear of the *Samantha D*'s massive hull.

The ten-foot drop to the ocean felt endless, a frightening plunge down a bottomless pit. Impact was harder — and colder — than Aiden expected. Suddenly, he was submerged, his gasps for breath drawing frigid salt water into his lungs.

The icy blast got him swimming. He broke the surface, choking and spitting. "Meg!" he cried. *"Meg!"*

The second syllable had just passed his lips when a whitecap broke over him, a hammer blow that drove him under again. He kicked with all his might and popped back up, looking frantically for his sister.

What he saw instead were waves — big ones — a fluid mountain range encircling him. The Pacific was alive, hurling fifteen-foot swells in every direction. Aiden was a tiny cork, bobbing helplessly, at the mercy of the titanic forces around him.

Where's Meg? Where's the raft? Where's —

Out of the darkness roared the hull of the *Samantha D*, hundreds of tons of metal hurtling toward him. Heart pounding, Aiden swung himself about in the water until his feet made contact with the wall of steel. Summoning all the strength in his legs, he pushed off, propelling his body away from the ship.

Through churning sea and spume, he felt his head bump into something soft and smooth. He glanced up, treading furiously to maintain his position against the wave action.

The raft! The ocean was tossing it like pizza dough, but — amazingly — the craft had landed right side up.

Now to find Meg . . .

All at once, something grabbed him from behind. The rush of instant horror was unlike anything Aiden had experienced before — a fright so basic, so primal, that it overwhelmed fear of capture and even fear of death. What could be worse than drowning? To be torn to pieces by a man-eating shark.

He tried to scream, but no sound would come out. Dread had robbed him of all wind. He wheeled in mute panic to face the monster that would end his life. . . .

Meg.

"What are you doing?" he rasped.

"Rescuing you!" she shouted, struggling to keep her head above the liquid chaos.

Aiden turned his attention to the raft. "Where's the door on this thing?"

Circling the craft in search of a way in proved nearly impossible. Each wave tilted them into a desperate upstream sprint. Then came the trough — a wild descent into the guts of the Pacific. Both were good swimmers, but exhaustion came quickly. Aiden grabbed a fistful of Meg's shirt to keep her from drifting away. He clung to her, but the effort made swimming impossible.

An awful sense of wonder came over him. Right here, right now, fatigue was more deadly than any shark. Soon there would be no energy left in them. They'd be at the mercy of the swells.

Unbelievable! We're going to drown three feet from the life raft. . . .

13

Aiden wrapped both arms around Meg and squeezed. The United States government had not been able to pry them apart; the ocean would not succeed, either. Whatever their fate, it would happen to them *together*.

The next wave struck hard. But as the Falconers tried to ride it, a second swell blindsided them at a ninety-degree angle. Aiden felt the collision as a rocket booster — an irresistible force that launched the siblings straight up.

They broke free of the water, and for an instant they seemed to hang there, suspended above the furious ocean. Aiden waited for the sea to grab them and drive them under — a dive from which they'd never recover. There was no energy left in them to fight this enemy. They were going down for good.

Whump!

They struck solid rubber. Aiden looked around in bewilderment.

The wave tossed us right onto the raft!

The hatch was just a few feet away, flapping wildly in the gale-force winds. He pushed his sister through it and scrambled inside, zipping the canopy behind him.

He collapsed to the waterproof floor, landing face-first in a pile of life jackets. "Quick!" He shrugged into his own vest and helped Meg into hers.

"Won't make — any difference," she managed to say, her speech interrupted by the chattering of her teeth. "If the — raft sinks, we'll die of hypo — thermia."

"Never thought I'd be colder than in the tank." Aiden shivered. He tried to embrace Meg to preserve body heat, but the frigid wetness of their clothes made that pointless. "We'll dry off sooner or later. Just keep the flap shut!"

"Are you kidding? I wouldn't go back out there if the Death Star was landing on our roof!"

Without warning, the inside of the raft lit up like a baseball stadium at night. Shocked, Aiden and Meg scrambled to their knees and squinted through the plastic window of the canopy.

The conning tower of the *Samantha D* loomed over them, about twenty yards off. Two powerful floodlights cut through the storm, trained on the life raft.

"Oh, come on!" Meg howled in frustration. "They're sitting on a billion gallons of stink oil that needs to be in Seattle! Why can't they leave us alone?"

"We've got to get away from that ship!" Aiden agreed urgently.

"How?" she demanded, slightly hysterical.

"With these!" Aiden pulled a pair of oars from behind the food stocks. "Come on!"

He unzipped the flap, and the two poked their heads out into nature at its most violent. Soaring waves sent white water cascading high in the air, where it mingled with the lashing downpour to form an icy liquid atmosphere. They began paddling madly.

"Don't beat at the water!" Aiden called. "Pull with your whole body!"

But he knew it was no use. A hundred oarsmen couldn't propel the raft in these conditions. They might as well have been rowing with wet noodles.

A swell broke over them, and the interior of the life raft was suddenly awash.

They heaved with every ounce of dwindling strength they had left. All their efforts had crystallized into this one impossible moment. There would be no Falconer family if their escape failed. This raft *had* to move.

"**W**hat's going on here?"

Captain McNicholl stormed the wheelhouse of the *Samantha D*, his strides easy and confident despite the bucking of the deck.

Bergeron peered through binoculars into the floodlights' glare. "We've got 'em, skipper," he said without looking up. "They won't get away — not in these seas."

"*Who* won't get away?" he demanded.

"The kids! They attacked Lopez and took off in one of the inflatables. Let's move closer, Mr. Drury — "

"Belay that!" snapped the captain. "Hard to starboard! Veer off!"

"No!" The first mate turned on his commander. "We can put a boat in the water! Bring them in!"

"In these conditions," McNicholl insisted, "we'd just as likely ram them."

"Those are the Falconers!" spat Bergeron. "The *traitors*!"

"Their *parents* are the traitors," the captain pointed out. "Those two are children."

"They tied Lopez up with duct tape!"

"Because they're desperate. I won't risk their lives — if they haven't drowned already."

The first mate's face radiated deep outrage. "How can any loyal American let them go free?"

"Any loyal American," the captain interrupted, "should be asking himself why our government pushes children to the point where *this* is their only option." He snatched the binoculars from Bergeron's hands and gazed into the floodlights' brilliance. The raft seemed like a tiny bouncing bottle cap, pummeled by storm, swells, and spindrift.

"Radio the Coast Guard — we'll keep the raft in sight till they get here. And tell them to bring divers." McNicholl paused, his face a thundercloud. "There may be a couple of bodies to recover."

Meg paddled furiously, commanding herself to ignore the searing agony in her arms and shoulders.

No pain . . . no storm . . . no ocean . . .

In her mind, she was in the backyard with Mom and Dad. The oar was a shovel, and they were digging up sod for a vegetable garden.

A faceful of spray jolted her out of the fantasy and very nearly knocked her over. Sputtering, she willed herself back to the yard.

When the *Samantha D*'s blinding floodlights dimmed a little, Aiden and Meg had thought the life raft was in motion at last. But their celebration was premature. The *ship,* not the raft, was changing position — retreating to watch them from a safe distance.

Without warning, the powerful beams winked out.

"It's about time — " she began.

And then horror robbed her of her voice. The lights hadn't been turned off; they'd been blocked from view —

By a wall of water thirty feet high!

"Back inside!" shouted Aiden.

They dove for the flap. Meg got there first. She scrambled through the opening and wheeled around to pull her brother to safety.

The monster wave broke. Five tons of sea came crashing down on the life raft with the destructive power of a small earthquake.

The force was like nothing Meg could ever have imagined — as if a hand the size of a Mack truck had covered the raft and pushed it deep under.

The ocean roared inside the small craft, sweeping the oar from her hands and bowling her over. Now a lethal projectile, the paddle struck the side of the canopy, swung up, and cracked her on the back of the head.

The impact tore through her. She saw one last thing before everything went dark and the raft filled up with water. . . .

It was her brother, overpowered by the fury cascading down on him, losing his grip on the life raft, and disappearing into the boiling blackness.

14

Aiden tumbled down the face of the wave, sliding into the lightless trough. Then — underwater, diving deeper, the pressure hurting his ears, heading for the bottom, the end —

A sudden rush of buoyancy lifted his head and shoulders up and out.

The life jacket!

He sucked air, choking on salted lungs. *"Meg!"* he howled, spinning around in a floundering search pattern. The raft was nowhere to be found.

His heart folded inside out. Sunk? Or was it just hidden behind the towering skyline of whitecaps?

The next swell drew him up its slopes. Desperately, he tried to use his temporary vantage point to search for the craft. Nothing. Even the floodlights of the *Samantha D* were little more than a distant flicker on the horizon now.

"Meg!" The ocean fell out from under him, and

he was on the way down again, careening to a dunking at the bottom.

He popped up once more, coughing and spitting. How long could he go on like this?

The answer was both comforting and terrible: *If I can stay conscious, the life jacket will never let me drown.*

But there were other, scarier possibilities. For all he knew, the current was carrying him out to open ocean.

"Are you out there, Meg? Can you hear me?"

There was no reply, only the brawl of gale and sea. Aiden rode the roller coaster, battered and scrambled, discombobulated, and finally, numb.

Agent Emmanuel Harris stepped off the plane into the Seattle-Tacoma airport, reeling from turbulence and bad airline coffee. The pilot blamed it on a huge offshore storm system — the bumpy ride, not the coffee. Harris could only imagine what conditions were like aboard ship in this weather.

He was reviving himself at the Starbucks stand when his cell phone rang. It was his assistant in Washington. Bad news, as usual.

"What do you mean, *overboard?*" Harris bellowed. "They fell off?"

"They *jumped* off," came the reply. "They tied up a sailor and escaped in an inflatable life raft."

Not for the first time, the FBI man was aware of a strange, almost fatherly pride. Those Falconers had to be the most daring, resourceful, and fearless kids in human history. The dark circles under his eyes testified to that.

A quick glance out the window at the blowing wind and rain brought him back to earth. "Is that safe?"

"Not according to the Coast Guard. They've got people on the scene, but no sign of the raft. There's not much chance of finding them until the weather improves."

"And then?" he demanded.

"There are two ways it can go. Search and rescue, or recovery. Search and rescue means the kids are probably still alive. Recovery means — "

"I *know* what it means," the agent interrupted. "Call me the *instant* you have news. Got that? You don't finish typing a sentence; you don't sharpen a pencil; you don't pause for a deep breath. When *you* hear, *I* hear."

It was the first time in a fifteen-year career that Emmanuel Harris had said no to a cup of coffee. He stepped out of line, bent double by the bag of shot puts that had materialized in the pit of his stomach.

Come on, kids. Hang in there.

After the brutal Pacific night, the early morning sun reflected off a surface that was flat calm, almost mirrorlike, broken only by the scattered ripples of jumping fish.

The swamped raft hung low in the sea, barely a pimple on the glassy plain. The support pole had collapsed, so the canopy covered Meg's sleeping form. She lay on her back in three inches of briny water. Had she toppled onto her stomach when the oar struck her, she almost certainly would have drowned.

She might have slumbered much longer if a tiny killifish hadn't jumped in through the flap, landing on top of her life jacket. Finding itself suddenly high and dry, the hapless creature began bouncing on her chest and face.

"Five more minutes," she mumbled, and then rolled over into a snootful of cold salt water.

Choking, she tried to leap up, and very nearly capsized the small craft. "Aiden!" she cried, struggling against the rubber of the canopy. All at once, her head poked out of the opening, and she remembered.

The raft. The escape. The storm.

And her brother, washed out to sea.

She hugged herself against a surge of horror and noticed the life jacket she was still wearing. *Aiden had one, too.*

But could a few pounds of flotation save him from the wrath of the world's mightiest ocean?

It can and it did! He's alive.

She believed it with all her heart — because the alternative was just too terrifying: Her brother drowned; Mom and Dad locked away forever; and Meg all alone in this heartless, unfeeling world.

He's alive, she repeated to herself. *I just have to find him.*

She took stock of what she had. The raft, plus assorted survival equipment. The food was intact, although the first aid kit was waterlogged — soaked bandages and seasickness pills reduced to mush.

I'd give anything for a dry sweater, she reflected with a shiver. She touched a sore spot on the back of her head, where the oar had conked her. *And some ice for this egg.*

She pulled an awkward-shaped object out of the pocket of her wet jeans.

Frank Lindenauer's opera glasses.

Eagerly, she panned the vast surrounding water

with the slightly fogged lenses, hoping against hope to see her brother bobbing and waving.

No Aiden.

The sting of disappointment was eased by a discovery that was almost as welcome: land. A lush green stripe of coastline, not too far away.

Her dilemma: paddle for shore or stay on the water to search for Aiden?

Meg thought it over. What were the odds that her brother would just happen to float into sight? She'd have a better chance of spotting him from land, where she could climb a hill or a tree for a clearer view.

Besides, it didn't help Aiden if they were *both* lost at sea.

When she picked up the oar, the entire right side of her body curled into a paralyzing cramp. *Oh, yeah, I did this about twenty zillion times last night.*

She began to row for shore, gritting her teeth in pain. However much this hurt, it had to be better than what poor Aiden was going through — floating and freezing in a life jacket. She paddled at top speed for a month and a half — at least it felt that way. It was probably more like an hour. The coastline seemed no closer.

This was going to be more of a marathon than she'd thought.

Aiden's voice echoed in her head: *Don't beat at the water. Pull with your whole body.*

"Know-it-all," she muttered aloud.

He wasn't even here, and he was distance-nagging her on sculling style. Aiden did everything by the book. According to Mom and Dad, he was the only six-year-old ever to learn to ride a bike by reading the manual.

Where does he get off lecturing me?

Suddenly, she was rowing with power and rhythm. The raft slid smoothly through the water at a pretty good clip.

The madder I get, the better I row!

All she had to do was think about things that made her angry. Rod Bergeron, Agent Harris, Hairless Joe — this was going to be easy!

Next stop: dry land.

15

Sun.

Aiden could only sense its presence. He hadn't seen it or anything else for hours.

Am I blind?

No, the salt from the ocean spray had cemented his eyelids shut.

He didn't mind the fierce rays that were burning through his hair to his scalp. Most of him was submerged in cold water. This was warmth, and he'd take it any way he could get it. Sunstroke was tomorrow's problem.

If there's such a thing as tomorrow for me.

Logic told him there wouldn't be. Rescue seemed about as likely as winning all fifty state lotteries on the same night. He was a tiny dot in the largest body of water on the planet. No one would ever find him.

I'm going to die.

Funny — he had faced death more than once in the past weeks, but always in split-second situations.

This was the first time he'd had a chance to *think* about his fate. In fact, thinking was just about the only thing he *could* do. He had squandered his strength fighting the storm last night.

Was it really last night? It feels like days. . . .

Only his brain still worked — and he wasn't even so sure about that. He had a very clear memory of a long conversation with Meg in the water, bobbing side by side in their life jackets. That was impossible. Meg wasn't with him. She'd stayed on the raft, hadn't she?

Please, please, let her be safe on the raft! She's Mom and Dad's only chance now.

Of course, that would mean Aiden was seeing things. Not a good sign. Hallucination was a textbook symptom. Thirst, hypothermia, exhaustion, and sun poisoning were wearing him down.

I could be dying already.

Meg just rolled her eyes and said, "You think too much, bro."

No! You're not here! He wanted to scream it out loud, as if volume might somehow make it true. But his mouth wouldn't open. It was on the fritz, along with his arms and legs.

There had to be some way to prove that his sister wasn't treading water beside him. That she wasn't about to share his gruesome fate. That she would live on to fight for the Falconer family.

So he told her the one thing he had never told her — that he never *would* tell her, because it was too dreadful to be spoken to another living soul.

"Meg," he said, and this time his lips did move, although his voice was barely a whisper, "sometimes I wonder if the reason no one ever found evidence Mom and Dad are innocent is because they're really guilty."

He waited for her to pound her fists against him, calling him a monster, an ungrateful, disloyal son. All were insults he silently unleashed upon himself in those ghastly moments when he lost faith in his parents' cause. But coming from Meg, the attack would cut deeper, sting more painfully. Never once — even for a fleeting instant — had his sister doubted that Mom and Dad were one hundred percent innocent.

Floating there, he waited for what seemed like a very long time. There were no blows, no angry words. Just the caw of gulls and the distant lapping of gentle surf.

He would have cheered if he'd had the breath. *She's not here! She's got a chance! Go, Meg!* Despite his fatigue, his clenched fist broke out of the water, punching feebly at the air.

Wrapped up in celebration for Meg, it never occurred to him to wonder what the sound of breakers might mean for him. He was mostly delirious when his feet struck sandy bottom. He couldn't walk, not really. Instead, his jelly legs churned in a weak bicycle motion, and he crawled blindly out of the Pacific onto dry land.

His fist was still balled in triumph for his sister when he collapsed to the beach into a sleep so deep that he didn't truly understand he was still alive.

When the raft bumped against the shore, Meg nearly wept. It had taken most of the day to reach land. Life on the run had made her tough. But nothing could have prepared her for the agony of rowing. The pulsing ache felt like it was alive — a throbbing, angry tapeworm, growing and claiming more and more territory in her tortured muscles. After the first couple of hours, the pain had spread from her right side to her left. Now it extended from the top of her head to the tips of her toes. Even her hair hurt.

The urge to sleep for a week was so powerful that

she had to slap herself awake. This was no time to relax. Her work had just begun.

She took in her surroundings. This part of the coast — Oregon? Washington? — was wilderness. Just in from the beach, tall trees and dense foliage began. The nearest town could have been half a mile away or a hundred.

No five-star hotels, she thought wryly. *Guess I'll have to live in the life raft for a while.*

It made sense. It had supplies, food, and water — she slapped at a mosquito — and the canopy would come in handy in this bug sanctuary.

There was only one problem with the raft. The crew of the *Samantha D* knew about it, which meant the authorities would be searching for it. A giant blob of fluorescent orange was hard to miss.

Hide it in the trees?

It was the smart move, but her muscles revolted. The thing weighed a ton. She and Aiden had barely been able to get it over the rail of the ship.

She took out all the equipment and supplies, carrying armloads of gear into the cover of the forest. Then she heaved the empty craft on its end and rolled it into the woods. The brush was so dense that she had to squeeze the bulky raft in between bushes and trunks.

Fugitive logic: *If I can't see the beach, someone on the beach can't see me.*

As soon as the water was no longer visible through the foliage, she set the life raft down flat in a small clearing. It was so tight that the inflatable sides pressed up against the surrounding trees. A few minutes later, she had retrieved the provisions and equipment.

Oh, how she would have given anything to avoid what was next. To have a chance of spotting Aiden, she had to gain altitude.

That means climbing a tree.

Biting her lip, she peered up the long, stiltlike evergreens. The gnarled maples around the Falconer home were so broad and overgrown that a handhold or foothold always seemed to be there when you needed it. But these fir trees were straight, narrow, and very tall. This was going to be like scaling a flagpole to the moon.

She selected a sturdy trunk and shinnied up it, her damp sneakers digging into the bark for traction. Her progress was better than she'd expected — which both impressed and alarmed her. Thirty feet above the forest floor, she was nowhere near the top.

Don't look down.

She climbed on. She'd have to get a lot higher than this for a clear view of the ocean.

As she ascended, whole vistas opened before her eyes. It was breathtaking — lush green hills rolling into the mountains to the east.

But not half as breathtaking as the swaying of this stupid tree!

Gasping, she clung to the bark and prayed for the wind to stop blowing. *Don't look down . . . don't look down. . . .*

She did, though — and immediately regretted it. This was at least double the elevation of the cargo crane in the Port of LA. Fall from here, and she'd be very, very dead.

She pressed her foot against a droopy limb that cracked under her weight. For a terrifying instant, she was slipping, sliding down the trunk like it was a firehouse pole. Her elbow struck the broken branch, sending a stab of fire up her arm. The pain almost caused her to let go. Whimpering, she held on, squeezing the tree as if trying to insert herself into the wood.

Deep breath. *Fall off a horse, get right back on again.*

Climbing more carefully now, she eased herself up the big fir until she was just a few feet below the top. She could make out a cluster of houses and buildings three or four miles inland — a small town. That was good to know. A town meant transportation. Once she and Aiden were reunited, they would have to find a way to Denver.

You're getting ahead of yourself. . . .

Gingerly, she shuffled around the trunk until the huge expanse of Pacific blue stretched before her. Feet set on a branch, her left arm in a hammerlock on the treetop, she reached down with her free hand and plucked the opera glasses from her pocket.

Do I really have a chance of noticing a tiny bobbing head in this vast ocean?

These past weeks had trained her to believe in miracles.

16

The tiny island had been deserted for a long time. Once a part of Cape Lookout State Park, the narrow sand spit had been cut off from the rest of Oregon by a storm back in the 1960s. Now it stood alone, empty, unclaimed by the Parks Department. There was no ferry service from the mainland. It was a forgotten place, without even so much as a name.

On the eighth of September, two backpackers took a small motorboat from Cape Lookout to explore what appeared to be a mound of trees growing out of the ocean itself. The cay they discovered was very much like the state park they had just left — low and rugged, with dense stands of pines.

The backpackers decided to hike to the shore and picnic overlooking the open Pacific. The trek turned out to be shorter than they'd expected — the little island was barely a football field wide.

It was the first, and by far the smallest, of their surprises that day.

There, sprawled on the beach, was a teenage boy, caked with salt and sand. He wasn't moving.

The man reached him first.

"Is he dead?" the woman asked in a tremulous voice.

The man rolled the body over. The face was lifeless — sunburned the dull pink of volcanic rock. The man bent low, his ear barely an inch from the victim's blistered lips.

"He's still breathing, but it's faint." He regarded the life jacket. "This kid went overboard somewhere. We've got to get him to a hospital."

The woman pulled out her cell phone to dial 9-1-1. "There's no signal."

"Go back to the bay side and try from there," her companion ordered. "He's dehydrated — who knows how long he's been lying here?"

As she ran off into the woods, the man produced a sport bottle and held it to the castaway's parched mouth. The water dribbled down his cheek.

"Drink," the man ordered. He forced the lips apart, allowing a trickle to creep between them.

The boy choked on it. Yet even those few drops of water brought him a half step back from his world of darkness.

Thirty minutes later, when the helicopter appeared above the island, Aiden Falconer was just conscious enough to hear it coming.

Water, Meg thought in disgust. *Big deal.*

Who said looking at water was restful? Whoever it was couldn't have been hanging off the top of a million-foot tree. If he had been, he'd have known that looking at water made a person have to go to the bathroom. Which meant a million-foot climb down and a million-foot climb up again.

Wait — what's that?

The opera glasses fixed on a dot amid the light ocean chop.

Please let it be him! Please let it be Aiden!

The dot spread white wings and took flight. Unless Aiden had learned to fly, this wasn't him.

For at least the twentieth time, she swallowed bitter disappointment. She could no longer contain the feeling that had been rising inside her ever since she'd awoken in the raft that morning.

For the past two days, she had been up and down this tree, scouring the coast, scanning the beaches. She'd checked every single whitecap, scrutinized each gull and pelican.

If Aiden hadn't gotten here yet, he might not be

coming at all. It was time to face the possibility that he might have drowned.

Stop it. He's not dead. He can't be dead. We have too much to do.

But the dreadful logic kept intruding on her hope. For two days, she had searched, living in the rubber raft, freezing through the nights, crunching gross dehydrated meals, and hiding from any boat or plane that might have been the Coast Guard.

Two days was a long time. *He should be here by now! The same tides and currents that brought me should have brought him, too.*

So where was he?

She summoned all the strength that was a part of her character. She would not — *could* not — admit that her brother was dead. That would have broken her. And falling apart was a luxury she did not have.

Aiden had always been right about one thing — Mom and Dad were all that mattered. She had to carry on the fight to prove they were innocent.

Even if that meant carrying on by herself.

The thought turned her to stone. Throughout this nightmare, it had always been Aiden and Meg — in the foster homes, the prison farm, and over these insane weeks on the run.

Now it would be just Meg.

Nothing, not even Mom and Dad's fate, had ever been sadder.

She clung to her perch, watching the sun set in a fireball. As it had twice before, the blue water blackened. She began to make her way down the tall trunk. She was getting better at this, but her tree-climbing career had come to an end.

Tomorrow she would head for town, find a way to get to Denver, and continue on their vital quest.

She had never felt more alone.

17

Aiden came back to himself as if crawling out of a deep sinkhole. He noticed the smell first — a sharp antiseptic odor, like in a doctor's office. Next he was aware of the oxygen feed in his nostrils and the IV tube in his arm.

A hospital? "Where — "

As his vision slowly returned, a dark shadow loomed over him. "Aiden!"

Why is that voice so familiar? "Who are you?"

"Where's your sister?" the voice demanded.

Aiden struggled with his own hazy perceptions. He'd been just about to ask the same question. All at once, his blurry focus sharpened into the features of a face straight out of his worst nightmares.

Agent Emmanuel Harris of the FBI.

Despite his weakened state, the identification made him sit bolt upright in bed. He retreated from his family's archenemy until he was pressed against the headboard with nowhere to go.

"Where's your sister?" Harris repeated. "Where's Margaret?"

"What makes you think I'd tell you?"

But it was a good question. A chaotic flood of memory came roaring back at him. Their escape from the *Samantha D*, the storm. The last time he saw Meg, she was clinging to the inflatable raft against the onslaught of waves as tall as houses.

Anything could have happened. For all he knew, she had fallen off the life raft and drowned.

No. I was way worse off than her. If I survived, she survived.

But there was no telling where she might be. The sea had been like the inside of a washing machine that night. The raft could have washed ashore almost anywhere. Worse, Meg had no way of knowing where to find him.

She probably thinks I'm dead.

"Aiden, use your head," Harris commanded. "She's too young to be on her own. You have to tell me where she is!"

The truth was Aiden didn't have a clue. But he wasn't going to share that with the hated J. Edgar Giraffe. No Falconer would ever cooperate with this cold, towering monster.

Harris leaned in closer, blotting out the light. "Don't you care about your sister?"

"I care about my family."

Still, Aiden agreed with the despised agent on one point: Meg was tough, but she was only eleven. It wasn't right for her to be alone in a treacherous world that was doubly dangerous for anybody named Falconer.

And there's nothing I can do to help her. . . .

Surely this was the cruelest twist of them all. He had survived the wrath of the Pacific Ocean only to be delivered into the clutches of the man who had ruined their lives.

Meg hiked through the dense foliage, muttering under her breath and fuming.

Man, I hate the woods.

She had already tripped twice, twisted her ankle once, and nearly left an eyeball on a dozen branches and brambles. One of those scratches had opened up the scrape on her face. She could feel a trickle of warm blood on her cheek as she trudged along.

I must look like I lost a heavyweight fight.

Lost — that was another word that described her situation. The nearest town was only a few miles away. So where was it? She'd been walking all morning — unless she was going in circles, which was a definite possibility.

There's no such thing as a straight line when you're sidestepping a zillion trees.

Now she was so turned around that she had no sense of which direction was the right one. If only she had a compass.

Or — while I'm wishing for something I don't have — how about a bulldozer? Then I could flatten this dumb forest and see where I'm going.

It was pointless, she knew, to rage against trees when there were so many more important things to worry about. But the more important things would make her think of Aiden.

And I will — not — cry!

How many times had the two of them talked about their parents in prison, lamenting, "How could it be worse?"

Aiden, dead. *That* was worse.

She sucked in a breath. *I will — not —*

One surefire recipe for getting her mind off her brother — climb another tree. She had to figure out where she was going. The sun was already past its peak.

Partway up a big-leaf maple, she spied the little

town to the southeast. Somehow, she'd wandered north. She programmed the new direction into her brain and started out again.

It was tough going. Twice more she had to scale trees in order to adjust her course. It was late afternoon before she finally reached the first sign of civilization — a small cluster of summer cabins, mostly deserted.

A rusted bicycle leaned against a trunk at the edge of the clearing. Not exactly a private jet, but transportation nonetheless. Her feet were killing her. She brushed a spiderweb off the handlebars and swung a leg over the seat.

Both tires were flat and the frame was bent, making balance difficult. She pedaled for a few shaky yards before giving up. Walking would be faster.

Town, it turned out, was only half a mile away. The dirt road intersected with a paved one, and a right turn brought her into a small strip of shops, restaurants, and houses.

Most of the stores were closed. Apparently, they rolled up the sidewalks when tourist season ended on Labor Day. You could have safely fired a cannon down the main drag if not for the volunteer fire department. Dressed in heavy coats and boots, they were scrambling around a ladder truck performing some sort of practice drill. Otherwise, the place was quiet.

"Son?"

Meg wheeled around in surprise. An older woman in an Oprah Winfrey sweatshirt was watching her from the doorway of a small luncheonette. "Oh, sorry, I thought you were a boy."

"My summer haircut hasn't grown out yet," Meg explained smoothly. In fact, looking like a boy had been the whole point. At least, looking like anyone other than the fugitive Margaret Falconer.

That was when the Oprah fan got a better view of Meg's scratched and bruised face. "What happened to you?"

"Bike accident," she said, thinking of the rusty wreck she'd left back at the cabins. "I zigged when I should have zagged." She started to walk on.

The woman rushed over and took her arm. "You come back and get cleaned up. I've got a first aid kit behind the counter."

"Oh, that's okay. My folks'll be here to pick me up any minute."

But the Oprah fan was insistent. Meg was afraid that a stronger refusal would arouse suspicion. She allowed herself to be led into the bathroom and fussed over with soap, warm water, and antibiotic cream. It felt good, almost like laying down her burdens for a few minutes.

Left alone, Meg gave herself a quick sponge bath with paper towels, removing a layer of dried seasalt. When she emerged, she found a steaming bowl of vegetable soup and a dinner roll waiting for her at the counter.

She hung back. "I don't have any money."

"You don't need money," the woman said kindly. "That's the last of everything. I don't stay open for dinner in the off-season."

Meg hadn't felt truly warm since she'd lowered herself into the freshwater tank of the *Samantha D*. The soup looked like heaven. She accepted it gratefully, burning her tongue and not caring. She slugged it back in record time, using the bread to soak up the very last drop.

She felt almost human again and sat back on her stool, momentarily content. "That was great. Thanks," she called into the kitchen.

"Excuse me?" came the answering voice over the sound of running water.

And then, from the TV mounted above the cash register, Meg heard two words that juiced an electric current through her body:

". . . Aiden Falconer."

18

Meg turned her head so quickly that her neck made an audible click. There on the screen, medical personnel surrounded a hospital bed, adjusting IVs and plumping pillows. As they stepped away, the patient was revealed.

Aiden — *alive*!

The entire world faded into the background as that single fact went supernova in her brain. Somehow, her brother had beaten the odds. He had made it. Meg wasn't alone anymore.

"Aiden Falconer, son of convicted traitors John and Louise Falconer, was brought by Medivac helicopter to Tillamook County Medical Center and treated for hypothermia and severe dehydration. His sister, Margaret, has not yet been located and is feared drowned in the storms that swept the Pacific Northwest on Thursday night."

"But you didn't drown, did you?" The Oprah fan

had come out of the kitchen and was regarding Meg intently.

Meg took a shot at damage control. "Huh? I'm just waiting for a ride. That kid they found has nothing to do with me."

The Oprah fan slid a folded newspaper across the counter. It was open to page five, where the headline read FUGITIVE KIDS GO OVERBOARD OFF OREGON COAST.

There was a picture of the *Samantha D*, docked in Seattle. Below that were two photographs that had become all too familiar — Aiden's and Meg's mug shots from the Department of Juvenile Corrections.

Meg hesitated. She looked different now — but not different enough. She had been caught.

She was off the stool, sprinting for the door in a flash.

"Come back!" pleaded the woman. "Let me help you!"

But Meg was already pounding down the street. The last thing she needed was "help" from the Oprah fan. Regular people believed that the justice system was on your side and turning yourself in was the sensible thing to do. Regular people didn't know how the world really worked.

Meg had thought she was too dispirited and

weary to set one foot in front of the other. But the universe had changed. Aiden was alive, and she could fly if she had to.

Aiden had to give J. Edgar Giraffe credit. The agent was persistent. All day he stuck to Aiden like glue, leaving his side only for quick trips to the microwave to heat up a cup of coffee the size of one of the forty-two-gallon barrels the Falconers had stowed away in.

To be cooped up with Harris was special torture. At first Aiden resolved to utter not one word to the man from the FBI. But lying in a hospital bed was boring in the extreme. As the interminable hours droned on, Aiden realized that his unwelcome companion was planning to sit there forever, slurping coffee and waiting for the patient to let slip something that would help the feds capture Meg.

"You're some piece of work," Aiden accused. "It's not enough for you to wreck my parents' lives. You have to hang around to rub it in that I'm going to jail, too."

Harris leaned forward in his chair. "Well, let's take a look at the charges — arson, escaping federal custody, breaking and entering, grand theft auto, resisting arrest, passing counterfeit money — "

"I never did that!" Aiden interrupted hotly. "I helped you catch the guy who was doing it!"

"A Mr. Rodney Bergeron, first mate of the *Samantha D*, was arrested in Seattle for trying to pass a phony fifty-dollar bill," Harris informed him. "According to him, it came from you."

"Because he *stole* it."

"So you admit that," said Harris. "That's quite a rap sheet, Aiden. People with that kind of record *belong* in custody. Where do you expect us to put you — Disney World?"

"That's not right, and you know it!" Aiden snapped. "None of that stuff would have happened if we were home with our parents!"

"Your parents had a fair trial and were convicted," the agent reminded him. "You may not like it, but that's no excuse for breaking the law."

Aiden heaved himself up, dislodging the oxygen feed from his nostrils and tugging on the IV tube. "My parents were framed by Frank Lindenauer! And if you hadn't been so anxious to close the case, you would have found out *he* was working for a charity that was part of HORUS!" He regarded

Harris with loathing. "But no. You needed an arrest to show on Fox News. *That's* why my parents are in prison for life. *That's* why I've got a rap sheet. *That's* why Meg — " He fell silent.

Harris jumped on the opening. "*Where's* Meg? That's the most important thing here — making sure you two are safe! Don't you see that we want what's best for you?"

Aiden rolled over and buried his face in the pillow. "I don't think my family can take much more of what you think is best for us," he muttered acidly.

The agent shifted in the chair, recrossing his long legs. "What would you say if I told you I can reopen your parents' case? You give us everything you've learned about Lindenauer, and we'll devote the full resources of the FBI to finding the truth."

Aiden couldn't believe his ears. Was J. Edgar Giraffe saying he *believed* them?

"And Mom and Dad go free?"

"*If* we find enough evidence for a new trial, and *if* your parents are found not guilty, then yes, they go free."

The bubble of hope popped just as quickly as it had appeared. *He doesn't want to clear Mom and Dad. He just wants me to cooperate because he thinks I can lead him to Meg.*

How could Aiden let himself believe, even for a second, that the architect of all their troubles might be willing to help them? Stupid, stupid, stupid!

"Forget it," he mumbled. "Do me a favor — want what's best for somebody else next time."

"How can I convince you that I'm trying to do the right thing?" Harris asked earnestly.

Aiden said nothing. In his opinion, J. Edgar Giraffe stood a better chance of sprouting wings and flying to Jupiter.

19

He's alive! He's alive! He's alive!

The thought turbocharged Meg's engine. She was out of town in the blink of an eye, leaving the lunch-eonette far behind.

You've got to disappear in case the Oprah fan calls the cops.

She wheeled off the main road into the cover of the woods, running easily. Everything felt better with hot food in her stomach and the knowledge that her brother was okay. Even the trees and brambles that had tormented her before seemed almost friendly now — a safe hiding place from the prying eyes of the world.

She slowed to a fast walk, taking stock of her situation. Despite her relief, things were dire. Aiden was in the hospital, possibly hurt, definitely caught. Meg had to get to him, but how? The TV report said he was at Tillamook County Medical Center, but where was that? For that matter, where was *she*?

I don't even know the name of the town I just ran away from.

First priority: finding the right hospital. It couldn't be too far away. Aiden might have drifted up or down the coast a ways, but not hundreds of miles. This wasn't a big city with a dozen different medical centers. There was probably only one for the entire area.

Second priority: transportation. She had none, and no money for buses or taxis. If she tried to hitch a ride, that would arouse suspicion — especially since she looked like she'd been wrestling a grizzly bear.

If I ever get to the hospital, I'll fit right in — into intensive care.

It was there, chewing on her own bitter joke, that she realized how she might reach her brother.

She hiked north to the dirt road and followed it to the small community of cabins. The old bike was right where she'd left it, in the weeds at the edge of the clearing.

She picked it up and got on once again, pedaling in a wobbly circle. The bent frame made riding difficult but not impossible. For her plan to succeed, she didn't have to go very far, anyway.

She walked the bike back toward town. Shortly

before the paved road, she guided it into the woods. That was tougher going, navigating the ruined tires through underbrush over uneven ground. She struggled along, moving parallel to the main street, just inside the trees. There was the luncheonette, followed by a few other structures. The fire station was a hundred feet ahead. She could hear the shouts and commands of the firefighters as they performed their drills out front.

Wrestling the bike through the growth, she hauled it over a narrow ditch and leaned it up against the side of a candle and gift shop, now closed for the season.

Furtively, she peered around the corner of the building. She was watching the firefighters but kept an eye on the luncheonette as well. Had the Oprah fan turned her in? There was no police car parked at the curb, no uniformed officer taking the woman's statement.

Maybe she really wanted to help me. Maybe she'd be willing to drive me to Aiden.

That would be a lot easier than the harebrained scheme Meg had in mind.

She hesitated. *I should ask her. . . .*

She shook her head to clear it. Too risky. *Fugitives have no friends. Everyone is a potential enemy.*

One of the firemen stepped out of his boots, tossed his gear into a pile, and started up a blue pickup truck.

Meg stiffened like a pointer. *This is it!*

Crunching gravel, the pickup turned left, heading north. Breathing a silent prayer, Meg rode straight into its path.

It happened in a split second: The driver stomped on the brakes. The truck's bed fishtailed. Meg pedaled madly, propelling herself right in front of tons of skidding metal.

The side of the pickup slammed into the rear of the bike like a swinging bat connecting with a fastball. At the moment of impact, Meg hurled herself off the saddle and hit the pavement, rolling blindly away from the collision.

The next thing she saw was a wall of blue metal screaming toward her.

It was the worst kind of miscalculation — a fatal one.

Aiden will never know how hard I tried —

All at once, the truck lurched to a halt — six inches in front of her.

The frantic driver was out of the truck and at her side instantly. "Kid — what happened?" He took in the mangled frame of the bike and assumed her small body was in just as damaged condition.

Meg moved her arms and legs to make sure she wasn't as badly hurt as she hoped she seemed. "I didn't see you," she said feebly.

The rest of the crew of firefighters stampeded onto the scene, heavy boots flopping. One look at Meg and the command was passed along the line. "The ambulance!"

Within sixty seconds, they had Meg strapped to a shutter, with her neck immobilized. An old Cadillac ambulance pulled up, and she was loaded inside.

The driver of the pickup climbed in with her. "Don't worry, kid. County is only twenty minutes away."

Meg frowned. "County?"

"Tillamook County Medical — they'll take good care of you."

The firefighter could tell that his patient was relieved. She smiled all the way to the hospital.

20

The instant Emmanuel Harris stepped out of the room, Aiden began the count. He'd been doing it all afternoon. On average, it took the FBI agent one hundred eighty seconds to reheat his enormous Styrofoam vats of coffee. By Aiden's best guess, that meant sixty seconds to the nurse's pantry, sixty at the microwave, and sixty back again.

He removed the oxygen feed and pulled out the IV tube, wincing as the needle came out of his arm. He threw on his salt-crusty jeans and T-shirt right over the hospital gown.

. . . fifty-five . . . fifty-six . . .

Patience . . . how'd you like to run into J. Edgar Giraffe in the hall?

. . . fifty-nine . . . sixty!

He was out the door in a flash, not running, but striding at maximum speed. He had no clue how to find the exit, just a vague recollection of the building on the way in. This was a small facility, not a big hospital. A couple of lucky turns and he should be out of here.

. . . ninety-one . . . ninety-two . . .

He pushed through heavy doors to be greeted by a gaggle of idiot-faced relatives cooing through Plexiglas at a nursery full of newborn infants. Whoops — Maternity. He reversed course and tried another corridor, scanning the signs: CARDIOLOGY, PEDIATRICS —

Where's Reception?

. . . one-nineteen . . . one-twenty. . . . Harris would be leaving the pantry now, headed back to Aiden's room.

Don't panic. Keep walking.

Was that the entrance up ahead? His heart soared. But Harris might walk in on the empty bed any second now.

He veered around the front desk, praying that no one would notice his disheveled clothes. The exit was twenty feet away. He made for it, his body tensed, ready to break into a run at the sound of Harris's deep baritone voice.

It didn't happen. The glass sliders whooshed open, welcoming him to sweet, dusky freedom. He stepped out onto the roadway and jumped quickly back. An old-fashioned Cadillac ambulance hurtled up the drive toward Emergency, siren blaring.

The split-second delay was a costly one. An iron grip closed on Aiden's shoulder, spinning him around. He came face-to-face with a uniformed policeman.

"I'm an uncle!" he babbled, recalling the maternity ward. Meg was the expert at excuses on the fly, but he had to try something. "My sister had her baby — I'm going to buy chocolate cigars — "

At that moment, six-foot-seven inches of indignant FBI agent came barreling through the main doors. He relaxed at the sight of Aiden in custody, but his anger did not dissipate.

"I took it easy on you because you've been through a lot. That stops now. Ever been in arm restraints before? Feels like you've been nailed to the bed." To the officer, he added, "I want a cop on every exit straight through till morning. Got it?"

"I'll tell the sheriff," the man assented.

Harris marched his prisoner back inside.

Why do they need to guard the doors when I'm in restraints? Aiden wondered. *How can I make a run for it if I'm strapped down?*

The answer struck him — Meg. They expected

her to come after him. All at once, he understood why Harris had been so anxious to let the TV station do a story on him. It was a trap — a trap for the one Falconer they hadn't caught yet.

And I'm the bait.

To Meg's eyes, Tillamook County Medical Center was a suspended ceiling and fluorescent lighting. She was still immobilized against the fiberglass shutter and could only stare straight up.

Two volunteer firefighters carried her inside. The driver of the pickup was one of them. "Entering Emergency," he informed her. "Approaching the admitting desk."

This running commentary had begun about thirty feet from the scene of the collision, right over the wailing of the siren. It was obvious the young man felt terrible and held himself responsible for the accident. He had no idea that Meg had orchestrated the whole thing.

The concerned face of the nurse leaned into Meg's field of view. "MVA?" the woman asked.

"Motor vehicle accident," the driver explained to Meg.

"It looks worse than it is," Meg told her. "You don't have to keep me glued to this surfboard."

More to the point, how was she going to look for Aiden when she was trussed up like a turkey?

"The doctor will be the judge of that," the nurse said sternly.

Soon Meg was on an examining table, still strapped to the shutter, waiting for the attending physician. He showed up a few minutes later — a hurried, frazzled internist with twelve hours of work to cram into an eight-hour shift. He checked her for broken bones and concussion, treated her scrapes and contusions, and gave her a shot of antibiotic to prevent infection. Ouch.

Meg didn't argue. Health care was a rare luxury for fugitives, and God only knew she needed some. There was very little chance of the doctor recognizing her. Somehow, the man managed to examine her without ever really looking at her. He wouldn't have known the difference if she'd been an injured baboon. He was finished and gone in a couple of minutes.

The nurse stuck her head into the room. "Be with you in a sec, hon."

That sec, Meg realized, was her window of opportunity to get out of there. The medical part of this visit was over. When the nurse returned, she would be armed with nosy questions about parents and insurance and hospital bills.

The time to take off was *now*.

Meg bolted down the hall and through the doors that separated Emergency from the rest of the facility. She was in the heart of Tillamook County Medical Center. Her brother was here somewhere.

But where?

21

Aiden gave up struggling against the restraints after a few minutes. Harris was right. It really *was* like being nailed to the bed. It wasn't a torture device — the straps were soft enough and didn't cut into his wrists. But there was no give in them whatsoever. Here he was and here he'd stay, until somebody decided otherwise.

"I warned you," Harris said mildly.

"You're a real hero," Aiden seethed. "You're a regular Justice League when the bad guys are locked away or strapped down, and you've got backup guarding all the doors."

"You're making a mistake treating me like the enemy," Harris informed him. "Did it ever occur to you that those cops are there for *your* protection?"

"Protection from what?" Aiden snorted. "They should be protecting me from *you*!"

"In case you've forgotten, there's a certain bald man with a grudge who keeps turning up in unexpected places, trying to kill you and your sister. What makes you so sure he won't go after Margaret? What makes you think he won't come here?"

Aiden couldn't hide his surprise. "You know about Hairless Joe?"

Harris was amused. "We're the FBI. It's our business to know things."

"Like you knew about Frank Lindenauer? He's a terrorist, and he framed my parents!"

The agent looked him squarely in the eye. "I intend to get to the bottom of that. That's the truth, whether you believe me or not. But a fat lot of good it'll do your family if you and Margaret get killed. Give your parents the choice — life in prison or two dead kids. What do you think they'll pick?"

Aiden made no reply. On that issue, J. Edgar Giraffe was exactly right.

Harris read his hesitation as secrecy. "Do you know something about that bald guy? Who is he? Why is he after you?"

"He probably hates our family," Aiden shot back. "Because everybody hates our family — thanks to you."

Harris sighed. "All right, don't cooperate. I just hope you realize I'm on your side before it's too late."

They lapsed into a long silence. Aiden was torn. He couldn't get over the feeling that on some level this tall rangy fed was trying to help.

Are you crazy? He's J. Edgar Giraffe! He doesn't care what happens to us. He just wants another promotion.

Yet everything the FBI man had told him was ringing true.

Held in place by the wrist restraints, he studied his captor's face. Harris looked like he hadn't slept since last Christmas. He was probably younger than Mom and Dad, but his face was lined, and the bags under his eyes were drooping toward his knees. His clothes were rumpled, and his entire posture was bone weary.

I guess this chase is almost as exhausting for him as it is for us. Aiden took some small satisfaction from that.

He watched in amazement as Harris's eyelids began to droop. The agent slipped a few inches lower in his chair, stretching his long legs halfway to the door.

Aiden couldn't believe it. Was he falling *asleep*? On the job?

It wasn't exactly snoring, but a regular rhythmic breathing began to issue from Harris's open mouth.

There was no question about it — he was *out*!

Aiden wanted to howl his agonized frustration to the four winds. J. Edgar Giraffe was dead to the world. There could never be a better chance for Aiden to recapture his freedom.

And he was tied to the bed.

Meg crept down the corridor, wound hardball-tight by a mixture of fright and frustration. She'd been all over this lousy hospital, risking discovery with every step out in the open.

Think! Would the police put a captured fugitive in a ward with other patients? No, and definitely not in a pediatric ward with kids.

They're holding Aiden alone somewhere.

That's what she needed to find — a private room with a cop at the door.

A cop. She was going to have to get past a police officer. She knew instantly that fast-talking wouldn't work. The CNN report had made that clear. The authorities were looking for her.

Her brow knit. She could never overpower a fully grown adult.

Ambush, then. I'll sneak up and whack him over the head.

The thought made her nauseous. The Falconer siblings had broken the law many times to keep their quest alive. But except for self-defense against Hairless Joe, they'd never had to harm anyone before.

She ducked into a supply closet. No way was she going to knock a police officer unconscious without some kind of weapon. Her eyes fell on a portable oxygen tank. She picked up the narrow cylinder. Perfect — no sharp edges, solid, but not so heavy that it was likely to do any permanent damage.

She selected a dinner plate from a shelf of dishes and cutlery. A crude plan was taking shape in her mind. Frisbee the plate into a wall, and when the cop came to investigate — *wham*! Not exactly a chess-master strategy, but it just might work.

She found a posted layout of the hospital labeled EAST WING. Patient rooms were marked with small pictures of beds. The wards had six or eight each. Farther down the hall were smaller squares, with a single bed each.

Bingo.

She memorized the course — two left turns and a right. The fear was nothing short of mind-blowing. The oxygen cylinder seemed to swell in her sweaty palm until she felt like she was holding a missile.

She peered around the corner. The corridor was empty. A sign read ROOMS 101–136. This was the place. But there was no cop.

Should I throw the plate to draw him out?

No — not yet . . .

Her pulse a drum solo, she began that long walk. She was totally exposed now. If anyone stepped out into the hall, she'd be a sitting duck. Without the element of surprise, she wouldn't have a prayer.

Every time she passed a doorway, she expected to be accosted, grabbed, arrested.

It can't be this easy. . . .

One seventeen — the first private room. Barely daring to incline her head, she peered sideways through the open door. There was a man in there — at least she thought it was a man. He was encased from head to toe in a full body cast, suspended on the bed by a system of wires and pulleys. Two haunted eyes gazed out at her from holes in the plaster.

Creepy. But at least this unfortunate wasn't likely to come after her.

She kept going, checking doors on both sides. Patients, the occasional visitor — her heart did a genuine backflip.

In an armchair in room 109 sat the last person Meg had expected — or wanted — to see.

Agent Emmanuel Harris of the FBI.

22

Her high-voltage panic triggered a flight instinct as basic as anything in the animal kingdom. The reaction was instant: Danger became escape. She pounded along the hardwood, past the body-cast man, away from the private rooms.

Jazzed with adrenaline, she wheeled around the corner, brandishing the oxygen tank. Fight or flight? That was the question.

Then she noticed something. Hers were the only footsteps. Holding her breath, she doubled back and peeked down the hall. No Harris.

Had the agent simply not seen her?

Impossible! He was in a chair facing me!

Her sneakers scarcely touching the floor, she retraced her steps to room 109. The doorway beckoned like the mouth of some pharaoh's tomb, promising untold rewards but also unspeakable danger. Trembling, she inched toward it. Maybe she'd been mistaken before. Maybe that wasn't really Harris. . . .

Oh, sure, like it's possible to misidentify an eight-foot-tall cop you watched and hated through every second of Mom and Dad's trial — and who starred in your every nightmare since.

She squinted into the tiny gap between the open door and the frame. Yes, it was him, all right. And Aiden in the bed, looking miserable, but healthy. Thank God for that, anyway.

She did a cartoon double take worthy of Bugs Bunny. J. Edgar Giraffe was slumped in the chair, fast asleep!

No. The world didn't work that way. This was too good to be true. Some kind of trap.

If the situation hadn't been so deadly serious, she might have laughed out loud.

Silently, she stepped around the door into the room. Aiden very nearly cried out at the sight of her, gesturing frantically at the dozing Harris.

I see him, she thought irritably. Overjoyed as she was to be reunited with her brother, she couldn't avoid a stab of annoyance. *Like I could overlook a slab of meat the size of a bull moose.*

She noticed the restraints that held Aiden down.

The straps looked complicated. If Harris woke up while she was busy freeing Aiden . . .

Take care of J. Edgar Giraffe first.

Reluctantly, she reared back the oxygen cylinder, ready to slam it down on the agent's skull. Aiden was so horrified he very nearly lifted off the bed, restraints and all. He shook his head vehemently, mouthing the word "no."

Wasn't that typical Aiden? To be weak at the very moment they had to be strong. This — Harris, asleep — was a *gift*. A stroke of luck when luck was in woefully short supply for anybody named Falconer.

Does he think I'm enjoying this? Braining a sleeping man? If I hit the creep too hard, I could fracture his skull. Maybe even kill him. It's something I wouldn't want to do to my worst enemy!

Of that, Meg was certain. There was no question that right now Emmanuel Harris *was* her worst enemy.

She swallowed hard and began to swing the instrument down. And froze.

A glint of light reflected off something metal hanging out of the agent's blazer.

Handcuffs.

She hesitated. *You could be throwing away Mom and Dad's last chance at justice.*

Safer to knock Harris out. He'd probably be fine. It was certainly no more than the big jerk deserved.

Yet a basic decency deep inside her — and Aiden's silent pleas — prevented her from striking the blow. They were the Falconers — the good guys, no matter what people said about them.

You don't cause injury when there might be another way.

She dropped to her knees and set the cylinder and plate gently on the floor. Meg had always been a good pickpocket. She'd once swiped her father's wallet right out of his pants to pay the Domino's delivery guy. Absorbed in a Mac Mulvey writing marathon, Dad had been totally clueless until a steaming slice of pizza had been waved under his nose.

With the touch of a surgeon, Meg twisted her index finger around the chain, slowly drawing the cuffs out of Harris's jacket.

Wait. Something's wrong. It feels too heavy. . . .

As the steel shackles emerged from the coat, she saw that a cell phone was wrapped in the chain. Suddenly, the handset came loose. With a lightning motion, Meg caught it just before it clattered to the floor.

She caught a petrified look from Aiden, but Meg's eyes were on Harris. The agent stirred, smacking his lips softly. She waited for the world to end.

It didn't happen. The big man resettled himself and slumbered on.

She stuffed the phone in her jeans and turned her attention to the cuffs. Where was the key? Barely breathing, she fished around the jacket as much as she dared. She pulled out an FBI badge and set it back inside like it was coated with acid. The mere touch of it burned her fingers. That agency had destroyed her family.

Car keys. Another piece of the escape puzzle fell into place. But what about the handcuff key? None of this was going to work if Harris could unlock himself.

Wait — what was this? She probed down with two fingers and came up with a small silver key.

Bull's-eye.

There was a radiator next to the chair. Meg took one cuff and fastened it around the heavy coil. Aiden's eyes were like saucers, but he never uttered a peep, silenced by awe and fascination.

The opposite cuff dangled over the arm of the sleeping agent.

One, two, three . . .

Meg snapped the shackle around Harris's wrist and squeezed with all the power of her anger against this man. The mechanism tightened with a series of clicks. Hard steel pressed into soft flesh, and he came awake with a cry of pain.

He leaped to his feet and was yanked back by the cuffs connecting him to the radiator. Meg retreated beyond his reach.

He gawked at her. "Margaret!" To her amazement, his first words expressed not rage but relief. "You're okay!"

"Okay?" In an instant, Meg had amassed enough rage for the two of them. "Is that what you think I am? Let me tell you something, mister. I am pretty far from being okay, and it's *all thanks to you*!"

Harris rattled the cuffs against the radiator. They held fast.

Meg was warming to her topic. "Our poor parents are rotting in jail; we almost got killed, like, fifty times — "

"*Meg!*" Aiden interrupted. "Undo these restraints so we can get out of here!"

"I can help you!" Harris pleaded, struggling against the shackles. "I *believe* you!"

She removed the strap from Aiden's left arm. "Then why are Mom and Dad still in prison?"

"It isn't that simple. I'm not the whole government — "

She pulled off the other restraint, and Aiden sat up. "Your face — " he began in concern.

Meg shrugged. "You can't hitch an ambulance ride without bleeding a little." She turned back to Harris, who had given up battling the cuffs and was riffling through his pockets with his free hand. She held out the silver key. "Looking for this?"

"I can protect you," the agent persisted. "You're not safe on your own!"

"I'm not the one with the radiator charm bracelet," Meg retorted. "I *am* clumsy, though." She stepped into the tiny bathroom, tossed the key into the toilet bowl, and flushed. "Oops."

That was enough for Emmanuel Harris. *"Emergency!"* he bellowed at the top of his lungs. *"Cop in trouble! Room one-oh-nine!"*

23

The Falconers exchanged dismayed glances. As long as Harris could yell for help, he was not yet defeated.

"Let's fly!" Aiden hissed.

They barreled into the hall, slamming the door urgently behind them.

"*Stop them!*"

The hospital was insulated for sound, so the foghorn voice was muffled.

But nobody can ignore that kind of hollering forever, thought Aiden, taking his sister's arm and dragging her away from the scene of the crime.

A nurse appeared in a doorway. She looked at them and then glanced farther down the hall in the direction of the ruckus. Aiden could see the uncertainty in her eyes. Should she detain the kids or see to the patient?

The caregiver in her sent her scurrying toward room 109.

The fugitives took off. A couple of quick turns and they were pounding toward the main lobby and freedom.

"Hold it!" Aiden wrestled Meg into a cleaning closet just before the reception area.

"What's the holdup, bro?" Meg rounded on her brother amid the mops and buckets. "I've got his car keys!"

"There's a cop outside the entrance," Aiden explained breathlessly. "He's already nailed me once."

"What about a different door?"

"They're at every exit — Harris's orders." Aiden could have kicked himself. *If I hadn't made that lame escape attempt, J. Edgar Giraffe never would have posted guards, and we'd be home free right now.*

"Climb out a window?" Meg suggested.

"They don't open wide enough." Aiden racked his brain. How could two kids get past cops who were there for one purpose — to stop two kids?

"Have you still got Harris's cell phone?"

She stared at him. "You want to call somebody *now*?"

Aiden took the handset, flipped it open, and accessed the call log. Sure enough, the display identified the last number dialed as TILLAMOOK CO. SHERIFF. He keyed it in quickly.

"Sheriff's office."

"This is the medical center," Aiden said in his deepest voice. "We've got your FBI agent hand-cuffed to a radiator in one-oh-nine." He broke the connection.

Meg was appalled. "Why are you helping Harris? We need all the head start we can get."

"Watch." Aiden opened the closet door a crack, and they waited. Less than a minute later, the uni-formed officer from the front door rushed by, head-ing for room 109. The coast was clear.

The Falconers were out the door and into the parking lot in a heartbeat. Meg was already poking at the door opener button on the keyless remote. There, by the driveway, stood a white Buick Cen-tury with rental car stickers, flashing its lights at them.

Meg tossed her brother the keys. "Still remember how to drive?"

He had only driven once before in his life — a stolen Chevy Tahoe from New Jersey to Vermont. Back then, he'd believed that his first experience be-hind the wheel would be his most desperate.

I was wrong.

He missed the driveway altogether and took sev-eral yards of grass with him as he hit the main road.

"I'll get better," he promised, stomping on the gas.

He had no choice. The only alternatives were getting caught or getting killed.

With an enormous two-handed heave, Harris pulled the steel radiator off its moorings. He stumbled backward and almost tripped over the startled nurse who had just rushed in the door. A jet of white steam exploded from the severed pipe and began to fill the room.

"What's happening?" she shrilled.

"Did you see two kids?" he bellowed over the hiss of rushing vapor.

Her glasses fogged over, and she had to take them off. "A teenager and a younger girl? They were heading for the lobby."

"Call Security!" He tried to pick up the radiator to carry it out of the room, but it was too hot to handle. "Ow!" He dropped it to the floor with a crash and dragged it into the hall. There, he nearly caused a collision of four Tillamook County police officers, converging from their posts at the hospital exits.

"Why did you leave your posts?" Harris demanded.

The oldest of the four spoke up. "The sheriff said you were handcuffed to . . ." His voice trailed off at the sight of the broken radiator dangling from the agent's wrist.

"They've got my car keys!" Harris raved. "Put out an APB on a white Century with Avis stickers! I need every man you've got to stop them before they get too far!"

There was an awkward silence, interrupted by the nurse's frantic call to Maintenance. "Hurry! The steam is coming out of the room and filling up the hall."

"Tell them to bring a hacksaw to get these cuffs off!" put in the FBI man. He turned to the four cops standing helplessly with their arms dangling at their sides. "Why isn't anybody going after those kids?"

"We have priorities, too," the senior officer explained. "We might be needed to evacuate patients if they can't turn off the steam."

"Then call in more manpower!" Harris raved. "Every second counts!"

"We *are* the manpower," the cop informed him. "Four on duty, one minding the store. That's it in the off-season."

Harris's broad shoulders slumped.

Those Falconer kids. They were getting away.

Again.

24

County Road G-114 was a cow path barely wide enough for the Buick. But it headed east, if the on-board compass was to be believed. And it definitely wasn't the kind of route where anybody would set up a roadblock.

Or so they hoped.

"We're low on gas," Meg commented.

Aiden shrugged. "Doesn't matter. We can't keep the car much longer. Everybody will be looking for it."

Meg swallowed hard and gazed out the window into the darkness. "I thought you were dead."

"I would have been if some hikers hadn't found me."

She nodded. "I know. I was about to head for Denver when I heard that on TV."

He regarded her in awe. "Denver?"

"Where else?"

He nodded slowly, gripping the wheel. She'd been ready to go to Denver. Alone.

His wild, impetuous little sister was the bravest human being he'd ever met. In the past year, her eleven-year-old world had been shattered and the pieces scattered to the four winds. Then, at rock bottom, with the one person left to her probably dead, she had still never wavered in the quest to free Mom and Dad.

She was *really* something.

"Denver, huh?" he repeated. "I guess that's where we're going now."

"You know it," she said stoutly.

When the cell phone rang, it was so unexpected that they both lifted off the Buick's front seat.

"Don't answer it!" Aiden said urgently. "It's probably Harris."

Meg frowned. "I thought he'd still be scuba diving in the toilet, looking for the handcuff key."

"We should toss the phone," Aiden decided. "There might be some way they can trace the signal."

"Good idea." She leaned sideways into Aiden at the wheel and held the handset out in front of their faces. "Say cheese." She snapped a picture with the camera function. Then she rolled down the window and pitched the phone into some trees.

The car never slowed down.

The phone came to rest faceup, its tiny sharp photo lighting the patch of weeds where it lay. Oddly enough, these were not the faces of two fugitives, crushed by exhaustion and defeat. The girl was angry yet triumphant, her tongue stuck out in defiance. The boy hunched over the top of the wheel, his determined eyes riveted on the task at hand, the road ahead, the future.

These were two young people who had seen the very worst of the world but were unbowed and unbeaten.

They knew what they had to do — and were on their way to do it.

Epilogue

The all-points bulletin on the latest escape by the young Falconers went out at eight-twenty-one P.M. Pacific time. The message was received by every police radio in Washington, Oregon, northern California, and western Idaho.

One of these receivers was in a small motel just outside Portland. The man in the room jotted down the details on hotel stationery: *White Buick Century, last seen at Tillamook County Medical Center*. He noted the number of the vehicle's Oregon license plates. Police procedures were familiar to him, although he was no cop.

Every officer who heard this APB would now be on the lookout for that car. The man in the motel knew he had to find it first. The Buick itself was unimportant. But the two kids inside it were of very special interest to him.

He ran his fingers over a head that was shaved

completely bald. The chase was on again. This time, he would not let the Falconers escape him.

It was the man Aiden and Meg called Hairless Joe.

About the Author

GORDON KORMAN began writing novels when he was a teenager and has been writing them ever since. His most recent books include those in the ISLAND, EVEREST, and DIVE trilogies, as well as *Son of the Mob*, *Son of the Mob: Hollywood Hustle*, and *Jake, Reinvented*. He lives in New York with his wife and children.

ON THE RUN

They're running for their lives... and running out of time!

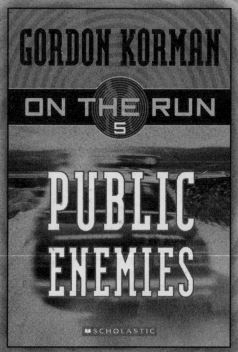

GORDON KORMAN

ON THE RUN
5

PUBLIC ENEMIES

■SCHOLASTIC

Aiden and Meg are running from state to state, searching for clues to prove their parents' innocenc. They're being chased by the FBI and an eerie killer known only as Hairless Joe. And the closer they get to the truth, the closer they get to danger.

■SCHOLASTIC